People pl

By Kay Hart

To Kay Hart

Cover by graphic designer, Louise Gillard

Acknowledgements

Thank-you Pippa, for the original idea and Phil., my long-suffering husband, for his technical support.
Also my Granddaughter Louise Gillard for her Art Work

Disclaimer

My story is totally fictitious, although the reader may recognise some place names. All characters are purely out of my own imagination and not intended to represent anyone alive or deceased.

People, Plants and Unicorns

Chapter 1. The Usual Suspects.

'Ere Miriam, did ee see that?' Betty, slipping back into her native Cornish dialect pointed to the yard outside the double shop doors near the till area.

'Did I see what?' asked Miriam.

'I'd swear he's at it again, old Malc; I've just seen Mrs. Peters hand him a fiver and he's gone and stuffed it into his sock, while loading a bag of compost into her trolley. Now they're headed for the car-park!' Betty pressed a button on the till for a read-out of recent transactions.

'No, Malc. Can't tell me this time he's just been given a tip. There's no record here this afternoon of anyone buying just one bag of compost.'

'You never know,' Miriam sighed, 'he might just hand it over when he's finished helping Mrs. Peters.'

'Hmmp!' snorted Betty; 'Any road, you and I have got all these houseplants to unload and display. Better get on with it while it's quiet.'

The Unicorn garden centre and coffee shop was a popular village attraction for both villagers and visitors to Cornhaven. Many years previously it had been the site of The Unicorn public house plus a small nursery growing tomatoes and lettuces in the summer months and chrysanthemums and freesias during the winter.

That was before Sir Arthur Wilberforce – Smythe had gone on a buying spree, wanting to add more land to his post-war empire, along with the almost derelict pub. It made a good garden centre site close to the Hampshire coast, about eleven hundred acres in all, extending into woodlands at the back, which was where Sir Arthur built his eight – bedroomed family home. The largest of the old greenhouses was converted into a shop opening out onto a generous sized yard for plants, compost, pots and landscaping materials.

The old Unicorn pub. Had been modernized to provide office space for Sir Arthur's grandson, Jeremy, who now ran the business, plus storage and staff – rooms. The addition of a conservatory for houseplants and other tropical plants plus a water gardens area and the coffee shop added to the attraction.

Sir Arthur and his son, Terrance Wilberforce-Smythe, were no longer around, but Terrance's wife, known to all and sundry as Lady Jane, liked to have her say, especially when it came to choosing new staff.

Mostly Lady Jane stayed in the background, but sometimes one or more of her old friends, or to be exact ladies saying they knew her, would turn up in the garden centre demanding personal shopping attention and expecting heavy discounts.

It usually fell on poor Betty's shoulders as shop supervisor to inform them that goods could not be discounted. The 'Everything's on computer' explanation mostly worked, but not always.

The houseplants were displayed in the added-on conservatory close to the tills, so the shop staff could watch for customers as they unpacked three trolley loads of cardboard boxes of plants.

'Do you think we should talk to Jeremy 'bout Malc?' asked Miriam.

'Dunno,' Betty replied. 'Let's wait a bit longer

and see what happens.'

'Righto,' said Miriam, 'suits me. When's Clive in again? Malc. Behaves himself if he's got the student working with him.'

'Should be back tomorrow. Finishes his written exams today,' Betty answered.

The two women worked their way meticulously through the boxes, checking invoices and looking for any sign of damage. Miriam enjoyed displaying the larger houseplants first; Monstera, Rubber plants, ferns and palms, and houseplants in hanging pots, which she hooked over a bar running the length of the conservatory.

Betty enjoyed the fussier work, displaying smaller flowering and foliage plants to perfection, after first making sure the display benches were immaculately clean.

Once supervisor Betty was satisfied with the display, she returned to stand guard over the tills while gentle, dark-haired Miriam cleared away the cardboard boxes to the yard recycle area, returning the metal trollies to the staff only part of the yard, hoping that just maybe Jeremy was out there, or at least working in his office over-looking the yard.

At thirty-eight, Miriam could still pass for eighteen, the age of her daughter from her marriage to David, so tragically killed in a motorway accident five years previously.
Daughter Joanne had now gone off to university and Miriam missed her company badly.
The garden centre work suited her. She enjoyed working with plants rather than endlessly tidying shop goods on the shelves.

Tom was the main plants person at the Unicorn, very knowledgeable, but well past sixty-five and due to retire any day soon Miriam had a talent for planting up outdoor displays, hanging-baskets and pots, working with Tom on community based projects around the village and nearby town, when time allowed.

Miriam harbored a desire for the plant supervisor's position when Tom retired, but had already been told 'No.' Jeremy wanted a horticulturally qualified person to replace Tom, especially as Jeremy's own qualifications were in business and finance, not horticulture.

So, Miriam resigned herself to looking after plants and customers, although she was allowed to give the odd demonstration, showing off her skills planting up display pots and baskets.

The staff had not yet been informed that interviews had already taken place. Jeremy and Lady Jane had made their joint decision and Tom's successor was about to be offered the position.

Malcolm was in his usual position in the yard under the covered compost sales area, watching two men from 'Perfect Pots' unpack and display a selection of large terracotta planters in the yard.

'Hi Malc, See you've got Bill and Ben in the yard again,' joked Alan, as he crossed the yard from his 'goods in' shed on the far side.

Malcolm grinned, 'and a good job they're doing too! Jeremy's doubled the order this time, as the pots sell so well. Nice stuff, mind you. Might buy a couple myself.' Malcolm offered Alan a cup of tea from the flask he kept under the covered area.

'Are you on for going to the dogs this Friday?' Malcolm asked. ' The wife's taking Alice to her grandparents' for the weekend, so I thought maybe we'd have a lads' night out. Young Clive's up for it.'

'Why not,' replied Alan. 'I'll look forward to it. There's food too, I think, all included in the ticket price. Had a smashing burger last time we went. Have you said anything to Tom, or Piers and Lucas in the pond department?'

'Tom's off somewhere with his missus and the other two, well, I suppose it's not really their thing, or Jeremy's, for that matter. But the three of us will enjoy it, won't we?'

'Definitely!' Alan replied. 'Best get back to work, got a lorry load of Tom's plants due any time and I need to make sure he's in the yard to check them off, all those Latin names! See you soon.'

The staff used mobile phones restricted to the garden centre only. No-one liked the system. It could be especially difficult when trying to advise one customer outdoors and being summoned by Betty to see another one waiting at the shop till.

Malcolm was with an elderly couple looking at paving slabs on the landscape materials side of the yard when he was called into the shop, where a customer wanted help moving a statue they had just purchased from near the shop doorway.

After apologizing to the couple in the yard, he went across to see Betty's customer, to help her move the heavy statue on a trolley, out to her car in the car-park across the driveway.

Pausing outside the shop doorway, he looked up and was horrified to see the couple in the yard making off with a stepping-stone paver, virtually running to the car-park. Before Malcolm and Betty could reach them, they'd loaded it into the car boot and drove away at speed without making any attempt to pay.

'They must have known I was on my own today.' Malcolm said. 'any other time I'd have Clive or one of the part-time staff with me.'
Betty was too stunned to speak at first, but eventually remarked 'But they looked such a NICE old couple. Who'd have thought it? And where are Tom and Alan?'

'Taking delivery of a load of plants round the back,' Malcolm replied. 'Isn't it always like it?'
Miriam returned from the coffee shop, where she'd been helping Julie clear up after a small child, who'd been sick over the floor.

'What have I missed?' she asked and Betty explained what had happened.

'Jeremy's out this afternoon,' Miriam said, 'but we really should let him know what's happened. At least we've only lost one stepping stone. I wonder what those people will do with it and if they'll be back again?'

Betty found the 'shop incidents' book' on a nearby shelf and wrote down details of what had happened.

Lauren

Lauren Harrison was sitting at her home office desk when the phone rang. She noted the number showing on the display and her heart missed a beat, as she hoped it would be good news.

'Mrs. Harrison?' the educated voice enquired, 'Lady Jane and I have decided to offer you the garden plant area supervisor's position here at the Unicorn garden centre, if you are still interested. I would really like you to start as soon as possible, before our current chap retires,' Jeremy continued.

Lauren hesitated for just a second before saying,' 'Yes, I'm definitely still interested and will be pleased to accept your offer. I'm free to start in two weeks' time, if that's OK with you?'

'Fine,' Jeremy replied, 'shall we say 9am on 5th May?'

'Thank-you, yes, I'm happy to go with that,' Lauren answered, just a little bit stunned. It would be only her second full-time job since her son was born. Oliver was now eight years old and with Mark, her husband running his own landscape business and able to arrange his own working hours, picking Oliver up from school could easily be arranged. Lauren was more than ready for a change from home life and looking forward to making more use of her own qualifications in horticulture and management.

It was her favourite time of year. She loved May month, seeing Spring slowly turn to summer. Her drive to work would take her past roadside verges filled with fresh leaves and wildflowers, from Bluebells and primroses at the start of the month to red champion, cowslips, foxgloves, cow parsley vetches and cornflowers later on.

Maybe not as spectacular as driving down through Devon and the South Hams where her parents now lived, but still lovely.

The Unicorn was just two miles from the Hampshire coast and about a half-hour drive from Lauren's home.

So, Monday 5th May found Lauren in Jeremy's office at the garden centre. It was Lady Jane who welcomed her and smiling wished her well. The signing-in system was explained and Lauren was given an issue of two polo shirts and a fleece jacket, in the company's colours of navy blue and gold. Lauren was relieved to see there were no 'can I help you?' type slogans on the clothes, just a neat, white and gold unicorn head with the words 'Unicorn Garden centre' embroidered around it against the navy material.

Lady Jane then handed over to Jeremy, who had just come into the office, to formally take Lauren to meet the rest of the staff.

Monday morning was Jeremy's regular staff meeting time, as it was normally fairly quiet then. Unusually for a garden centre, the Unicorn did not open on Sundays, due to some ancient local legislation from the previous business, so all the staff had Sunday free, plus one other weekday of their choosing, but worked alternate Saturdays.

After Lauren had placed her new uniform in a staff-room locker, she followed Jeremy across the yard into the shop, where Betty and Miriam were on duty. Malcolm and Clive were called in from the yard and Tom came in from the garden plants area, to be introduced to Lauren.

'Of course, this isn't everyone,' said Jeremy, 'altogether there are nineteen of us, Lauren. Over the next few days you'll get to meet our part-time staff plus Piers and Lucas who run the water garden department and I mustn't forget our wonderful coffee shop ladies, but today I'll leave you with Tom to go through the office side of your job, as well as familiarizing yourself with our current garden plants layout.

I expect you'll have some new ideas of your own, too?' With that, Jeremy headed back to his office above the staff-room, in what used to be the old Unicorn public house.

The supervisors shared a room with desks, computers, printers and two mainline phones situated next to the shop till area, with a window looking out onto the shop floor. Tom fetched down a large box file from one of the shelves. 'Right lass,' he started, 'here's lists of some of the nurseries supplying our plants, but they are also on the computer. Are you used to doing your own buying?'

'Sometimes,' Lauren replied, but when I worked for Glam Gardens most of the buying was done at head office for their ten centre's. But I do know my plants, am used to checking the quality and I know what makes a good deal from previous training programmes.'

'Sounds good,' said Tom. 'Just make sure you check and double check deliveries and invoices on arrival. We've got Alan in the yard to check the goods in when transport arrives, but he's no plant expert.'

'I'm really looking forward to getting stuck in,' said Lauren. 'Who will be working with me outside?'

'Well, there's Miriam,' Tom replied. 'Lovely lass, about your age and good with all the plants and customers. Then for help with the heavier loads there's Malcolm and our present student, Clive.

Malcolm's daughter, Alice, usually comes in on Wednesdays for work experience, but is happiest working with Piers or Lucas looking after the pond fish in their tanks, though sometimes we get her to help in the coffee shop. Lovely little lass, has Down's syndrome, but very bright. She is quite fond of Miriam and Betty too.' Tom seemed distracted for a few moments. Lauren asked him if anything was wrong.

He looked at her and sighed, 'Not my place to cast aspersions, Lauren, but just keep an eye on Malcolm. Betty says she's seen him hanging on to cash meant for the business, if you know what I mean. Sooner or later Jeremy will find out, but we're all so fond of Alice, and after all, Malc. Is her Dad.'

'Oh!,' said Lauren, 'I'll tread carefully with that one.'

'Right then,' said Tom, 'you know about the staff-room, I expect. There are lockers there, if you want one, though most of us tend to live out of our own cars. We have got a bit of an enclosed yard just for staff, if you want to eat your lunch outside and we can buy food in the coffee shop in our lunch break at a discount too.'

'What's in the old glasshouses round the back?' asked Lauren.

'Not a lot,' came the reply, 'but if you're into wildlife you'll see sand lizards scurrying around the ground under the old benches, especially in warm weather. In early spring the benches are used to grow some of the bedding plants we sell. This is very much Miriam's area. She plants up hanging baskets and pots for customers there through April and May. I think she's still working on Mrs. Grey's ten baskets at the moment. Miriam has a talent for it, used to have her own florist's business, back before her husband was killed, but that's another story.'

As if on cue, Miriam appeared in the office doorway.

'Lauren,' she began, 'there's a customer in the shop who would like to meet you. Her name's Mrs. Montgomery-Jacobs, says she's a friend of Lady Jane.'

Lauren stepped out into the shop feeling nervous. Mrs. Montgomery-Jacobs, a severe looking sixty something eyed her up and down before speaking.

'So you're the new gal, taking over Tom's role I believe? Now, you must know Lady Jane and I are great friends and I expect a good discount on my purchases here, at least ten percent! Today I want to buy those three dwarf rhododendron bushes by the shop door. Betty tells me they're £15 each. I'm not paying that! I'll give you £35 for all three.'

Lauren drew herself up to her full 5ft 4in height.

'Madam those particular plants were set aside for one of our special projects and are at their discounted price all ready. We couldn't possibly upset Lady Jane by telling her that a friend of hers thinks they are second quality and not worth the price she's asking, could we? But if you insist, I'll call Lady Jane and ask her myself.'

'No, no! Please don't bother her on my behalf, I'll pay the ticket price.' A crestfallen Mrs. M-J replied as she headed towards the cash desk.

Tom and Miriam grinned at Lauren. 'So what's the 'special project' then?

Tom asked. 'Don't know. But I would have come up with something,' Lauren replied. ' Right team, let's go sort some plants!'

The rest of the morning passed quickly, as the three of them worked through benches of bedding plants, perennials, climbing plants and shrubs, deciding which ones were past their best and could be discounted, as well as removing dead flowers and watering dry pots. There was an automated watering system, but as Tom explained, it did not always work very well, except on the lined-out potted trees, just coming into leaf.

Lauren was beginning to get some ideas on how she would like to change some of the displays, but not until Tom officially retired at the end of the week.

She had the greatest respect for the older man and was pleased to hear that he would still be busy working for Lady Jane as her gardener, as well as continuing various planting projects with Miriam, in her spare time.

Although, Tom was married to Susan, newly retired from working at the village nursing home, and she had plans too.

When Miriam headed off to the staff room for her break, Lauren asked Tom about her.

'Bit of a sad thing there,' Tom said. 'Miriam was married to Dave for thirteen years. Lovely guy, worked at Southampton airport. Then one day there was a terrible accident in thick fog on the M27, as he was heading home.

Dave didn't make it. Left Miriam with Joanne to bring up on her own, though Miriam's parents tried to help at the time. Child was just into her teens. Mind you, Miriam did a good job. Joanne's up at Manchester university now. Miriam struggled on with her floristry business for a while, but in the end was beaten by costs. Not a lot of money in it. So, she's been here about three years.'

'Thank-you Tom,' said Lauren. 'I'm certainly impressed by the way she works and hope she's not too put out by Jeremy employing me in this position. I'll do all I can to keep her happy here. Oh no, what's happening over there?'

Raised voices could be heard from the walled part of the plants area, where the climbers were lined out.

'Let's tackle this one together,' Lauren said to Tom, as they headed across the yard to where a young couple were looking through the line of climbing plants.

'Would you like some help?' Lauren began, 'Is there a problem with our climbing plants?'

'There certainly is,' snapped back the female half of the duo. ' I can't find a single plant here to do the job I want and your advertising states 'climbers for every situation.'

I need to hide some old fencing, about five panels to be exact. Just look at these descriptions. This label says, 'will grow up to two meters, this says up to four meters and so on. I don't want them to grow UP, I want them to grow ALONG!'

Tom tried hard not to look at Lauren, who seemed totally bemused by the woman.

' Madam,' he began, ' I'm afraid that doesn't just happen. Climbing plants do need training to spread in the direction you need them to grow. Please come and have a look at our honeysuckle growing near the entrance and I can show you how we've trained it to grow along the wall.'

'Oh I can't be bothered with all that,' the disgruntled customer replied, 'I think I'll just get some shrubs.'

With that, the pair of them turned and walked away.

'Wow, whatever next?' Lauren mused.

She was excited by the thought of being free to choose and buy plants for the centre, which would involve day trips out to see suppliers and visit trade shows for new ideas.

Meanwhile, as long as there was someone else in the outdoor department, she could spend some time working through availability lists and seeing just how many plants she recognized.

Piers and Lucas

Piers and Lucas were mostly left to their own devices running the water garden section of the business. Jeremy considered it to be an added attraction, encouraging parents and grandparents to bring children into the centre to see the fish. So far, just garden pond fish, but in the future they might just consider 'tropicals.'

Piers, tall, blond and always immaculately dressed, was the organizer half of the partnership, while Lucas, a little shorter and darker in hair and skin tone was the more artistic of the two, enjoying designing water gardens for well-to-do clients.

Both shared buying in the stock, which included some landscaping materials, such as pebbles, sand, gravel and statues, along with pond pumps, chemicals, fish food, water plants and cold water fish.

They thought of themselves as 'co-managers,' though Jeremy had resisted giving any member of his staff that title.

This particular Monday morning in May, Piers was stock-taking landscaping materials while Lucas worked on a new water garden design at his desk in their department. He looked up, as his partner stormed in looking extremely annoyed.

.'Had my suspicions last week,' Piers began, ' the figures Jeremy gave me this morning don't add up. We're at least £20 down on takings for landscape materials. I think SOMEONE is cheating on us.'

'Piers, are you really sure this time?' Lucas asked. 'If so, we've no option but to take it up with Jeremy. If it's who we suspect, it's young

Alice I feel sorry for, if it's proved to be her Dad pocketing the cash. Are they really that hard up?'

'What do you suggest we do?' asked Piers.

'Perhaps what we need is better security,' Lucas replied. 'I could approach Jeremy about a better camera system to cover our bit of the yard. In the meantime let's have a word with Lauren, the new plants person. She's worked for a bigger company in the past and should know what to look out for.'

'OK, but you're cooking dinner tonight! I can't face it after all this stress, snapped Piers.

'Green Thai curry, then?' Lucas grinned, before breaking off to serve some customers looking at pond pumps.

Having failed to find any further discrepancies, Piers had calmed down sufficiently by lunchtime to approach Lauren, who was heading towards the staff-room with Tom, having left Miriam in charge.

'Lauren, let me introduce you to Piers,' Tom began, 'he runs the water garden department with Lucas.'

'I've heard it's very successful,' Lauren replied.

'Most of the time,' Piers sighed, 'but we have a problem and I need your help. Stock appears to be going missing and we do have a suspect.'

'Don't tell me; I suppose it's Malcolm in the yard,' Lauren said. 'Do you have any evidence that it's definitely him?'

'Well, no,' Piers replied, 'I was hoping you might be able to give us some advice. I've thought about asking Jeremy for better security camera cover on our half of the yard.'

'Not a bad idea. Would you like me to put it forward, as I'm the 'newbie' here?' suggested Lauren. 'I can say I think it needs updating. In the meantime, perhaps we all need to be more vigilant, looking out for each other's stock, especially in the yard, which is quite open to the car park. If Malcolm is guilty, just letting him be included too in surveillance action might put a stop to any dishonesty on his part.'

Tom, who had been listening silently to their conversation, shuffled his feet nervously, 'Well, let's hope it can work, but it's a big area to watch all the time.'

In the end, it was Piers and Lauren who approached Jeremy together to discuss better security in the yard, without naming anyone else.

'There's never been a problem in the past, so I've never thought it necessary,' Jeremy began,

'but I will look into it and get some quotes. At the moment it is just the main gates and shop entrance that's covered. Leave it with me.'

After Piers and Lauren had left his office, Jeremy sat quietly thinking about what they had said regarding the business's security. He hadn't pressed them as to exactly why they were so concerned, but he did feel they were not telling him the whole story.

Soon it would be his regular meeting time with Noric, to give the annual report. Noric would be bound to sense if something was not right.

Glancing out of his office window, Jeremy saw Lauren speaking to Miriam outside the staff-room. Even wearing the garden centre's uniform, how attractive Miriam looked, but Mother would never approve, would she?

She'd never forgiven him for losing Caroline, the wife Lady Jane DID approve of. The marriage had lasted less than a year. Caroline did not want children, told Jeremy he was 'boring' and finally ran off to New Zealand with Eric, Lady Jane's own gardener at the time.

So, Jeremy buried himself in running the estate and the garden , which was doing rather well.

The security company confirmed that they would send someone out the following Monday to assess security needs for the garden centre, especially closed circuit television coverage. Something to mention at next week's staff meeting.

Lucas looked up from his drawing board as Piers returned to their department. 'How did it go?' he asked. 'You do seem somewhat calmer now.'

'Pretty good. Lauren's a wonderful help,' Piers replied.

'For now, we've all got to work together and just be extra vigilant. Jeremy is getting quotes for the extra security.'

'Good, that's settled then,' smiled Lucas. 'Soon be time to go home, and don't forget I'm cooking tonight.'

The Plot Thickens

Lauren, her husband Mark and their son, Oliver sat down to a fish and chips supper from their local chippy in Romsey.

'Well then,' Mark began, 'so how did your first day at the Unicorn go?'

'Fine, but I'm exhausted,' Lauren replied, as she went on to tell them both of the day's events.

When she'd finished, Mark looked thoughtful,

'You know I've quoted for three different jobs down near that garden centre, mainly hard landscaping, and got nowhere with any of them. I couldn't have charged less, but it's as if someone is undercutting me every time. My prices are very fair.'

'Can I help you, Daddy?' Oliver asked, 'it's my half-term holiday soon'.

'I'll think about it, Ollie,' Mark replied, 'but I still need to find another project to work on. At the moment Mummy will be bringing in almost double the money I'm earning with the business each month.'

By Wednesday, Lauren felt more settled into a routine. No-one had mentioned anything else going missing and she was looking forward to meeting Malcolm's daughter, Alice, due in on work experience from her school. Alice's mother, Jill, dropped her off sharply at 9am, as it was Malcolm's day off that week. Miriam and Lauren went to meet Alice and were greeted with a cheery 'Hello!' from the fifteen year old.

'Must go and see Betty,' Alice said, waving a £5 note in front of Lauren. ' I forgot this last week. A lady gave it to Daddy for compost, but it's not his to keep.'

'Oh! I see,' Lauren replied. 'Yes, let's take it in to Betty.'

Betty looked totally stunned as she accepted the £5 and put it into the shop till, after pressing the 'compost' button.

After Alice had skipped off to do some work with Piers in the water garden department, Betty, Lauren and Miriam met up in the conservatory, where they could keep a look out for customers in the shop and plants departments, while they talked.

'Tha's taken wind right out of my sails,' began Betty. 'Can't be Malcolm, can it?'

'Unlikely. I think we need to look further afield,' replied Lauren. 'Miriam, have you seen anyone at all acting suspiciously in the garden centre?'

'Do you mean customers or staff?' asked Miriam, ''cause none of us would steal from Jeremy. He's a good employer. I've known a lot worse.'

'The only thing that comes to my mind,' said Betty, 'is that old guy nicking seeds last month. Right under our noses, it was. Young Alice said she saw an old man with a small knife in his hand going through the rack of vegetable seeds.

Didn't make anything of it at the time. We see all sorts in here, THEN when we were stock-taking I found seed packets that were cut right through at the bottom, still hanging on their hooks, but the inner foil packets containing the seeds had all been removed! What a cheek!'

'How much did you lose?' Lauren asked.

'Oh loads; at least four packets of vegetable seeds. Mind you, he never came back again, did he?'

'Then there was the couple who stole the stepping-stone while Malcolm was helping Betty's customer,' said Miriam.

'Until we get the new security system,' Lauren began, 'is there any way we can be more vigilant ourselves?'

'It's fine when we've got the extra staff in, all the part-timers,' Miriam replied, 'but so difficult either end of the day, especially once they've gone home. I think any dodgy customers will have worked this out for themselves.'

Unknown to the ladies, Jeremy had entered the back of the shop and had heard part of their conversation, unsure what to do. Now he took the opportunity to approach them. ' Is there a problem, ladies?' he asked.

'Oh no, Jeremy. We were just thinking about how we could do more for shop security,' Betty replied.

Jeremy nodded his head. 'I've been on to the camera company and the new system should be up and running by the end of next week. In the meantime, let's all just keep our eyes peeled.

I've just come from the coffee shop. Julie and her staff will be organizing a retirement party for Tom this Friday, so if you would like to contribute towards a leaving present for him, please see Julie today. Is that OK with you all?'

'Yes Jeremy,' they replied in unison.
'Right then, back to work everyone!' With that, Jeremy returned to his office.

Tom's Retirement.

Friday afternoon soon came round. Jeremy had invited Tom's wife, Susan to drop into the coffee shop after normal closing, just after 5pm. Coffee shop supervisor Julie and two of her staff, Jan and Shirley were busily piling plates of sandwiches and pastries onto the tables, as the rest of the garden centre staff scrambled in through the door, closely followed by Jeremy with Tom and Susan.

Once everyone had found a seat and a cup of tea, Jeremy stood up, clapping his hands for quietness,

'Not sure how many of you know this,' Jeremy began, 'but today we are wishing Tom a very happy retirement after an amazing fifty years working firstly for my father on our estate and more recently being our plants guru here at the garden centre. He was just sixteen when he first worked here.'

Applause broke out amongst the twenty strong group present. 'I'm delighted to add,' Jeremy continued, 'that Tom has agreed to carry on helping my mother with her garden, for the time being. Lauren's been left with pretty big boots to fill, so I hope you'll all support her too. Now, Tom, I think Betty has a small present for you, so you won't forget us.'

Betty stepped forward carrying an engraved tankard, which she handed to Tom as she congratulated him, plus a huge bouquet of spring flowers, created by Miriam, which was handed to Susan.

'There is just one other little thing I thought you might like for your own garden,' said Jeremy.

'Please look outside the café door.'

Tom and Susan opened the door to the outside seating area, to be greeted by the sight of a beautiful, carved arbour seat, tied round with a large ribbon. They both had tears in their eyes, as they thanked Jeremy for all his kindness.

'It's just what we need, wonderful!' Tom said. 'Good, I'll ask Alan to move it down to your garden tomorrow, but for now, let's enjoy this lovely food. Oh, and later this evening you're all invited to free drinks at The Fisherman's across the road,' Jeremy smiled. 'See you there at 8pm?'

'You bet!' came the united reply.

So, later that evening found Lauren, Mark her husband, Miriam, Betty, Tom and Susan huddled around a window table in The Fisherman's Rest. Jeremy and Alan were in deep conversation on the opposite side of the room, surrounded by various others, including Piers, Lucas, Clive and Malcolm. Betty remarked on the 'male conclave!'

'You know,' Tom began, 'I've never seen Jeremy so happy and I can't get over his generosity to me.'

'Wellll,' Betty replied, 'I just MIGHT know something about that. The other day my daughter, Joy, was in our village post office talking to Rachel, you know, Eric's sister. Remember Eric running off to New Zealand with Jeremy's Caroline?'

'Well yes, so what happened?' Tom asked.
'There's been an accident out there,' Betty continued, 'The daft bitch insisted they went white water rafting. In MAY! Winter out there, because she was 'bored!'
Surprised they found a company to agree to it on South Island, very risky. Any road, came to

grief, didn't they? Eric just about survived and got rescued, but they couldn't get to Caroline in the raging water and her body was fished out downstream the next day.

I think in spite of the divorce, poor Jeremy always thought she might demand more money off him, but now he's free of the worry.'

There was silence at the table, followed by a

'Wow,' from Lauren.

'You never know,' said Betty, 'there just might be a bit more cash being splashed around the garden centre from now on. Watch this space!'

Tom had secretly been watching Miriam's reaction, smiling to himself.

Security.

The following Monday morning, Jeremy held a shorter than usual staff meeting, informing everyone about the plans for improved security to combat any shoplifting.

True to their word, Covert Cameras representatives, Jon and Giles, arrived with clip-boards at the ready, sharp at 10am. Jeremy decided it would be best to let the two of them carry out a survey on their own first, before making any decisions himself.

As well as positioning cameras, the security of various gates, fences and walling was to be checked.

The rough, partially graveled, track serving the garden centre, customer car park and finally leading to Jeremy and his mother's home was at right angles to the main roadside of the sales yard.

There was a separate entrance for deliveries to the left of the yard, with a fence separating the 'goods in' from the sales area.

Jon and Giles spent a full hour walking and surveying the boundaries, before moving inside the yard and finally going through the various areas in the shop and coffee shop.

At mid-day they met with Jeremy in his office. Giles had brought with him a sample camera and electronic tablet device, which Jeremy could use to view any camera display at any time he chose. They talked through how recordings could be made and saved.

Between them they decided on a total of twelve security cameras, with motion sensitive devices to be set on the main gates and shop entrance, active after the shop closing time.

Arrangements were made to have the cameras up and running by the end of the week.
Then Jon added, 'BUT, we think you may have a serious problem with the side entrance.'

' WHAT side entrance?' asked Jeremy.

' The one in from the lay-by on the main 'road?' queried Jon.

' But I thought that was sealed up many years ago,' said Jeremy. 'It's completely overgrown with ivy now, isn't it?'

'You'd better come out and see for yourself,' Jon replied.

The three men left Jeremy's office and headed out across the sales yard, through the hard landscaping section.

As Jeremy had indicated, the old wall and fencing on that side of the yard were thick with ivy, at least seven feet high.

With a sweep of his right arm, Jon lifted long trails of ivy to one side, revealing an old side door, going back to when the yard was part of the previous nursery.

The remains of an old chain and padlock hung to one side of the wooden door. Jon was able to make the door open inwards, without too much force.

'I would recommend a total replacement of this section of the boundary fence and wall for security,' he said, 'but in the meantime we could provide you with one of our 'special effects' security cameras to cover this area.'

Intrigued, Jeremy agreed and asked for further details of what they proposed.

On Wednesday, the electricians turned up to fit the cameras. Miriam had agreed to allow them some space to work from in the old glasshouses at the back of the centre, where she was busily completing orders for planted pots and hanging baskets.

She was pleasantly surprised by a visit from Jeremy, checking up on the work later in the day.

'Miriam,' he began, ' I'm seriously impressed by these lovely flowering displays. Our customers love your work and I know this is the third year some have brought their hanging-baskets back to us to be replanted by you. I'm planning a few changes, hoping to expand, just a bit to start with and I'd like to offer you the job of supervisor in charge of house plants and seasonal bedding plants, if you are interested? There would be a modest pay rise, of course, for the extra responsibility.'
Miriam was stunned.

' But you've only just taken on Lauren,' she replied.

' Lauren, if she agrees, will become overall manager of the outside plant area. So the two of you will still be working together. I want to make the most of her degree standard knowledge and will be employing some extra staff as well as taking on some students from Southampton college from time to time. What do you think? Are you interested?'

'Oh yes,' Miriam replied. 'I hope I won't let you down.'

'I'm sure that will never happen,' Jeremy replied. ' one of our main house plant suppliers has an open day coming up soon and I'd like to take you to see the nursery and new promotions. Will you come with me?'

'Yes, of course,' Miriam replied, aware of a strange fluttering sensation in her breast.

'Good, that's settled then. I'll let you know the

date tomorrow.' With that, he headed outside to inspect the electrician's work before returning to his office.

Alice had been standing in the yard with Malcolm, her father, watching the engineers fix cameras in various positions. ' I wonder if the van man's been stopped there today, Dad,' she said.

'What van man?' asked Malcolm.

'Just the other side of the wall. He's often parked there by the ivy. It's a big green van with white writing and side doors.

' Haven't you seen him too?'

'Can't say I've noticed, but it is just a layby, Alice. Anyone can park there. Perhaps he's eating his lunch in the van.'

'Don't think he comes to the café. Never seen him talking to Betty either. Must just be a busy person.'

Alice strolled back into the shop to see if Lucas wanted her to feed the fish before going home time.

Malcolm decided it might just be worth mentioning the green van to Jeremy. Two of the part-time staff were helping customers with compost, so he went over to Jeremy's office. After telling him about Alice's observations, he added, 'Of course, probably nothing criminal, but Alice often sees things I miss.'

'That's OK Malcolm, better to err on the side of caution's what I say. There will be a special security camera watching that area soon. So we'll just wait and see what happens. I know that Piers and Lucas have been concerned for some time about stock going missing, mainly ornamental white chippings and rockery stone.

Alan swears blind that last weekend he fork-lifted three pallet loads of stone round there, but on Monday less than two were accounted for. Just keep watch and let me know if anything else goes missing. In the meantime, I'll see if I can find out who owns that van, though it could all be perfectly innocent.'

With that, Malcolm returned to the yard. The men from Covert Cameras were packing up for the afternoon, returning tools to Miriam's glasshouse, saying they were confident in finishing the job the next day.

Miriam finished watering the newly planted pots and baskets and went to see if Lauren needed any help outside before closing, feeling excited about her new promotion.

Moving Forward

On the Friday morning, Lauren was in the shop office working her way through lists of available plants at the various wholesale nurseries on her lap-top. Sometimes there were photographs, sometimes just names and she liked to see just how many varieties she could visualize as the names came up for ordering for delivery the following week.

Shrubs formed the mainstay of the outdoor plants area. May was usually the busiest month for sales, with so many plants available and on the 'looking good' list. Both evergreen and deciduous shrubs were showing new growth, many with flower buds as well as new leaves.

Lauren liked to have shrubs arranged in A to Z order on the benches, to help both customers and staff find the plants recommended for any particular situation. She had plans for 'tweaking' the outdoor displays to attract interest. Perhaps 'container plant of the month' for a small table plus a special collection of coastal garden plants, with the Unicorn garden centre being only about two miles from the sea, as the crow flies.

As she scribbled down notes and typed in a few orders, Jeremy entered the office.

'Lauren,' he began, 'you'll be pleased to know that our new security system is finally operational and I'll be checking it out over the weekend. At your interview, I indicated that after Tom retired, your job title could change to 'plant area manager.' How do you feel about taking it on now? Will you accept it? I feel that already you're showing great promise for the business.'

'Yes. I'm happy to be recognized as a manager,' Lauren replied 'and there are certainly some changes or additions I'd like to make to my department. Miriam's told me she's happy to take over organizing the seasonal bedding plants, which is a good idea as she enjoys making up the pots and baskets for our customers, plus I believe she will be 'house plant supervisor?' Makes a lot of sense, especially bearing in mind she once had her own floristry business.'

'Good. That's settled then,' Jeremy smiled. 'I will be taking on extra staff to work with both of you soon. I've asked Miriam to go to the open day at our house plant suppliers' nursery with me and I'd very much like both you and Clive to go along to visit our main plant wholesaler's nursery near Littlehampton later this month.

Clive tells me he has a place at Bath University to study for his degree in Horticulture from September onwards. I believe you and Mark got your degrees at Bath?'

'Yes. That's where we first met. I'm pleased to hear that Clive's going there too. He'll enjoy the course. And I'll be happy to take Clive along to Littlehampton with me, Lauren responded.

'Oh, by the way,' Jeremy added, 'Betty will now be formally known as 'shop manager,' as she's more than earned the title over the past eight years or so, since I took over the garden centre. I've taken on two new girls to help with customer service and organizing the shop goods.'

'It sounds as though you're pleased with the business generally,' Lauren grinned.

'Very much so, very much so,' Jeremy smiled back, leaving Lauren to complete her ordering.

There appeared to be no further attempts at theft from the yard over the weekend. Betty and Piers were booked to go to a trade show to look at both Christmas gift ideas for the shop and new promotions for the water gardening department. Betty especially loved these events in Birmingham, although it was a very long day out, leaving before normal working hours and returning late in the day, but this year Piers had offered to do all the driving in his new car, so it wouldn't be so bad.

On arrival at the National Exhibition centre they would sign in, be given badges stating where they were from, plus carrier bags to take a myriad of advertising brochures and leaflets from the companies they needed to see.

Betty always returned bursting with ideas for potential orders but Piers was a lot more cautious, looking deeply into value for money and choosing just a handful of suppliers' stands to visit.

He was pleased, however, when offered free drinks and small gifts, one of which was a key - ring shaped like a pair of miniature hose connectors. Betty had some sample toys and a pen holder decorated with plastic red berries, by the end of the day.

There was another trip planned, purely to see Christmas gifts and displays from one of their main suppliers. They were both under strict orders from Jeremy NOT to place any orders at the show.

Lauren and Clive's' visit to Farplants nurseries was booked for early June. Miriam and Jeremy had arranged to see the house plant suppliers between the two May bank holidays.

Miriam was feeling quite nervous but excited about going 'over the border' into Dorset with Jeremy for the first time.

The day of Jeremy and Miriam's visit to the Dorset houseplant importers and wholesalers soon came round. Although Miriam had become accustomed to dealing with various suppliers when she had her own flower shop, this was the first time Jeremy had invited her to go along with him to a trade open day.

She had purchased new navy blue trousers and shoes to wear with her works' top and brand new supervisor's badge.

Jeremy smiled when he met her at the door of his office and could not resist being charmed by her slightly anxious hazel eyes and long, dark hair, which she wore loosely touching her shoulders. He grabbed his customary tweed jacket off the back of the door, before they both headed downstairs to his car.

Miriam chatted enthusiastically about her work, when questioned by Jeremy, as they negotiated the busy roads, saying how much she was looking forward to the visit. Jeremy was enjoying simply listening to her voice, saying how much he would appreciate her opinions on the variety and quality of the plants they were about to see, without placing any orders on the day. There would be deals to be done at a later date.

The houseplant wholesaler's open days were strictly for a limited number of the garden centre's and other retail outlets regularly supplied by them. No more than thirty individuals were invited to attend at any one time.

On arrival at the nursery, Jeremy and Miriam were offered coffee and biscuits after first signing in, in part of one of the large glasshouses cleared of plants for the occasion.

By mid-May, sales of houseplants usually dropped in favour of customers buying more outdoor and summer bedding plants, but there were still plenty of people wanting a flowering houseplant to give as a present or fresh foliage plants to decorate their home or work-place, to improve the atmosphere.

Miriam had gone through a phase, she told Jeremy, of collecting cacti and succulents, always looking for new varieties for a particularly hot, sunny window sill and now her daughter, Joanne, was carrying on the family tradition, taking two of her favourite cacti away with her, to university.

'You don't look anywhere near old enough to have a daughter at university,' Jeremy remarked, as he sipped his coffee and was surprised to learn that Miriam was just a year younger than himself.

Once all the invited guests or delegates had arrived, they were divided into groups of six, to be taken on a conducted tour of the nursery, which was mostly under glass.

Everyone had been given printed lists of available plants, with space to make notes of any they might want to buy. Jeremy and Miriam both decided it would be a good idea to put a tick against the names they were interested in and compare notes later.

The tour started with row upon row of huge foliage plants, including indoor palms, rubber plants, cheese plants and ferns, newly imported from Belgium, then they moved on to smaller pots which would easily fit into the average car boot. This was followed by benches of window sill or table top foliage and flowering plants, including orchids.

Finally they arrived at the hottest part of the nursery holding trays of cacti and succulents, all for indoor display, although it was explained that larger specimens of these plants could be used outdoors through the summer months in hot, dry weather. This idea was becoming more popular with people who liked container planting but also went away from home for long periods in the summer, as the cacti and succulents would survive without a lot of water.

Next they moved on to look round the huge packing shed, where they were shown how individual pots could be labeled and bar-coded, ready for sale, according to their destination.

Miriam was impressed, especially when she discovered that there was a system in place to rent out the larger, foliage plants for events and businesses.

She asked Jeremy whether he thought this might be possible to do at their garden centre. He was not at all sure, because of the condition the plants would be in when they were returned,

'If we did try this,' he said, we would have to charge a fairly hefty deposit. Do you think customers would be willing to pay, say renting plants for a wedding marquee or indoor event?' Miriam remained intrigued by the idea. She would soon be taking the nearby town hall hanging-baskets over to them and thought the committee just might be interested in some indoor plants as well, when organizing events.

Two hours passed very quickly, as there was such a lot to view and discuss. At 12.30 precisely, all the guests were invited into the nursery's large staff room for a buffet lunch. Miriam and Jeremy remarked on the generosity of their hosts when they saw the choices and amount of food laid out for them. Those not driving could even have a glass of wine, if they wished, along with a range of soft drinks, tea and coffee. Miriam was introduced to several supervisors and managers from other businesses.

A chance to compare notes on houseplant sales. Jeremy looked on, between chatting to contacts made at previous events.

By 2pm the invited guests started to drift away home. Jeremy and Miriam thanked their hosts profusely for what had turned out to be a very useful and productive visit, saying they were very impressed with the quality of the plants on offer - not a greenfly in sight anywhere!

On the drive back to the Unicorn, Jeremy seemed quieter and more thoughtful. Miriam assumed he had found the event tiring.

Eventually he suggested, 'Miriam, I think it would be useful if we had a get-together in my office tomorrow morning, just to compare notes on what we've seen today. Perhaps we could work together on future orders?'

'Yes, please. That would be brilliant.' Miriam replied with enthusiasm.

'Good. Shall we say 10am? As far as I know, I'm free then,' Jeremy said, smiling.

Meanwhile, Back at the Ranch - - - -

Malcolm and Betty were stood facing each other, either side of the shop entrance.
Malcolm had just finished helping Alan bring a pallet load of charcoal into the shop, to be displayed with the barbeques at the back.

Betty was watching two mothers with their two children wandering up and down every aisle in the shop. She recognized the four of them and just knew the bagged sweets stand would be where they would finally stop.

'Watch this,' Betty said. 'They come in every Wednesday afternoon and do exactly the same thing.'

'What's that?' asked Malcolm.

'You'll see,' Betty replied.

After much slow deliberation and arguing with the two children, one small packet of boiled sweets was selected and brought to the tills. The sweets were opened immediately they had been paid for and the children, a girl and a boy, allowed one sweet each, as the group wandered out into the yard, past Betty and Malcolm.

By the time the four reached the outside sales benches, the boy had finished his sweet and was begging his mother for a second one.

'NO! My lor lad, you can't have another one yet! You must learn to SAVOUR the sweet, not eat it like that!' his mother shouted.

'See what I mean?' said Betty, 'and it's exactly the same every Wednesday.'

'Blimey!' replied Malcolm, 'do you think they are really that hard-up?'

'Never seen them buy anything other than them sweets,' Betty replied.

'You're doing all right yourself now though.

What's it like being promoted to shop manager?' Malcolm asked.

'Lovely surprise, really, and it's good to have some extra help, though I seem to have lost Miriam, now she's houseplants supervisor. Out with Jeremy today, she is.' Betty sighed.

'Think there's anything going on there?' Malcolm queried.

'Welll, she is a bit sweet on Jeremy, but not in his class, is she? Then there was that spot of bother nearly thirty years ago now, in Cornhaven village hall, remember? When Miriam's mother and her anti-fox hunting cronies had a go at Lady Jane's husband when he ran the hunt committee?'

'What happened back then?' asked Malcolm.

'Well, there the committee was, meeting in the village hall and these women decided to sabotage the meeting with homemade petrol bombs. Didn't work out though 'cause one broke as they tried to break in through the gents' toilet window. One of 'em got burned, so that was that.
But I don't think Lady Jane ever forgave the village women for trying.'

'Wasn't it a hunt meeting that caused Sir Terrence's death?' asked Malcolm.

'That's right. His horse bolted when it saw the fox and threw him against a hedge. Broke his neck, poor chap and that was that. Should 'av stuck to playing golf.'

Lady Jane was having similar ideas to Malcolm, as she watched Jeremy and Miriam return to the Unicorn, leaving his car in the driveway. Looking down from one of the offices over the staffroom, where had met with accountant Jed to discuss various financial matters, she became aware of a certain attraction, perhaps more than just friendliness, between Jeremy and Miriam. Of course, nothing could come of it, she reasoned; Miriam was hardly one of the 'county set.' No breeding. But then, she had been proved so wrong about Caroline, who had seemed the ideal choice for a daughter-in-law.

Then there was that business with Miriam's mother and the anti-foxhunting brigade in Cornhaven.

But that was a long time ago and since Miriam lost her husband and was left to bring up Joanne on her own, Lady Jane felt a certain sympathy towards her. Good looking gal, that one and a hard worker. Just have to wait and see.

Lucas had something altogether different on his mind and needed to speak to Lauren urgently. He found her unpacking the last of three trolley loads of shrubs from Farplants nurseries, trying to create the space to display them to best advantage.

'Hi Lucas, what's up?' Lauren asked, straightening her back as she turned to face him.

'Interesting problem from one of my contacts,' Lucas replied, 'and I would welcome some advice. I believe you and Mark are both Royal Horticultural Society members and know all about the Chelsea flower show? Well, there's a chance I could be involved in doing a water garden display for one of the show gardens next year.'

'Wow! Wonderful news. How can I help?' asked Lauren.

'I need to also let the guys know my own ideas on suitable plants and where to source them. I know that, in a way, this is short notice, even though , there's a full year to go. It's Chelsea next week, isn't it? I hope to go there with Piers on the Saturday, just to get a better idea of what's acceptable.'

Lucas showed Lauren a rough sketch of his own idea for the garden, adding, 'The company putting it all together is hoping to promote a particular charity, I think one of our local hospices. A really worthwhile cause.'

'Mark and I won't make Chelsea this year,' Lauren replied, 'due to various work commitments, plus it's still a bit of a long day away for Oliver, as he's only eight. But I'm keen to help you any way I can. I'd be glad to list some plants that might fit in. This is a brilliant design. Hope you win the brief. Does Jeremy know about this yet?'

'No, I thought I'd run it past you first, to see if you think it's do-able. Hopefully the Unicorn might gain a little publicity. I'm sure Jeremy would approve if it all works out,' was Lucas' cautious reply.

Lauren became aware that they were being watched. An older man of shriveled-up complexion, short with beady-black eyes and carrying a notebook in one hand had appeared from behind one of the shrub display benches.

'Lucas, do you know that man?' she asked quietly.

'Oh yes, that's Jed, employed as Jeremy's business accountant. Been around donkey's years. Used to work for Sir Terrance, way back. You'll see him making notes all the time around the place. Likes to think he's into health and safety, too.'

Jed, realizing he'd been spotted, turned and scurried away.

'Weird!' said Lauren. 'Doesn't he ever speak to you?'

'Rarely,' Lucas replied, then usually only if he thinks something's wrong. We call him 'The Mole.'

'By the way, Lauren, hope you won't mind me asking, but we've heard you were working for the 'Glam Gardens' chain. Was there a problem with them?'

'No, not with them,' Lauren answered, 'it was me. I got quite a nasty illness during the time I was with them and ended up in hospital, paralysed.

Could have been Lyme disease from a tick bite in the New Forest, but the doctors weren't sure. It's taken me two years to get fully mobile again, but I'm more or less OK now, apart from some weakness in my legs. Lucky to have survived, they said. It's good to be back working, though I was able to help Mark from time to time with his landscaping business.'

A tall, thin lady, immaculately dressed in a neat brown suit, was scrutinizing the benches of perennial plants, obviously searching for a particular name amongst them.

Lauren's cheery 'can I help you, madam?' was surprisingly met by the woman bursting into tears.

'I've got to have it, but it's not here!' she cried. 'Purple Loosestrife; I must have Purple Loosestrife for my memories, for the anniversary!'

'I'm so sorry,' Lauren said softly, 'but Purple Loosestrife has not yet been delivered to us to sell. The plants have to reach a certain size before the nursery will send them out to us, with the rest of the wildflower collection. Come into the shop with me and if you're happy to leave us your name and a phone number, I can call you as soon as the plants come in.'

The woman dried her eyes, saying, 'Oh very well, I suppose that will have to do,' as they walked into the shop together.

By this time Miriam had returned and was busy, watering the houseplants and bedding plants, getting ready to pack up for the afternoon.

Lucas had returned to his desk and after she had written Mrs. Webb's request for Purple Loosestrife in the 'enquiries' book, Lauren returned to unpacking the remaining shrubs, checking them all for water, as she went.

She thought she could hear music, then realized it was Miriam, singing as she worked. Miriam had a lovely, sweet, melodic voice and along with her daughter, was one of the regular choristers at Cornhaven parish church. Her taste in music was wide-reaching and today she was humming a love song.

'Had a good day out with Jeremy, then?' Lauren shouted across to Miriam.

'Oh yes,' came the reply, 'and I'm meeting with him again tomorrow morning to discuss future houseplant orders.'

'Good for you!' responded Lauren. 'In a couple of weeks' time I'm off to Littlehampton with Clive to see our main shrub and perennial suppliers. Good to get out and about, isn't it?'

Questions and Answers

The following morning found Miriam, armed with her notes from the previous day's visit to the houseplant nurseries, arrive at 10am sharp to Jeremy's office. To her surprise, it was Jed who sat behind Jeremy's desk, with a stack of files in front of him.

'Ah, Miriam. Jeremy's on his way. I'm just going through some figures for his records,' Jed announced, a little sharply.

Miriam noticed the word 'Noric' on the top file and wondered what it meant.

'Oh, nothing to do with you!' Jed replied, 'It's the consultancy Jeremy goes to for business advice. He won't say exactly what or why, but I've worked it out. You see the letters, N.O.R'I.C? I think it stands for a well-known group of professionals, that is the National Organization for Retail and Independent Consultants. Makes sense, doesn't it?'

Just then Jeremy arrived for his meeting with Miriam. Jed jumped up, saying, 'I've just completed the figures you wanted, Sir,' as he scurried out of the office.

'Sorry, Miriam,' Jeremy began, 'I wasn't expecting Jed to be in today. I think my mother was looking into some of our outgoings with him. Anyway, back to houseplants. Have you thought about putting an order together for next week?'

They spent an enjoyable hour pouring over plant names and prices, discussing what would be looking at its best the following week and also be longer lasting, in case sales slowed down.

At one point, their fingers touched, as Jeremy

reached across the desk to look at Miriam's notes. She was aware of a certain electricity between them and blushed as their eyes met, before quickly looking away.

I think I can safely leave the houseplant orders up to you,' Jeremy smiled. 'Lauren will carry on ordering the rest, but please work with her when you need more bedding plants. Those hanging baskets in the old glasshouses look magnificent.

'Am I right in thinking some of them go out this weekend? All paid for?'

'Yes, Tom's coming in on Saturday morning to help me load the van and deliver the first fifty,' Miriam replied. 'Altogether, I've planted up over 200.'

'That's wonderful!' Jeremy exclaimed. 'I was wondering if, as a thank-you, you might consider coming out for dinner with me? Perhaps one evening next week? A friend of mine has opened a new restaurant in Bournemouth and I'm longing to check it out.'

Miriam was so stunned, she struggled to reply,

'Yes, I'd love to!' with her heart singing inside her, as she left the office.

Miriam decided to keep quiet about her dinner date with Jeremy; well, it would only create jealousy, wouldn't it?

But Lauren couldn't help but notice how distracted she seemed, as she returned to work with the bedding plants.

'Everything OK, Miriam?' Lauren asked.

'Oh yes, fine thank-you,' came the reply.

Lauren returned to where she had been working, sorting through a bench full of perennial plants and became aware of a group of four people, a tall, serious-looking man with three young women, examining each potted plant carefully.

Lauren had been told by Betty that the local college would send staff with students to study what was on offer at the garden centre, and this group fitted the description Betty had given.

The tall man, referred to as 'Steven,' by one of the girls in the group, zoomed in on one of the pots, pushing his thumb into the surface of the compost and pulling out a plug of fertilizer pellets.

'You see! This is just what I mean about garden centre's NOT caring for their plants!' Steven started. 'Look! Snail's eggs!.'
Lauren just had to intervene, 'I'm sorry sir, but that is a plug of fertilizer which is added to improve the health of the plant. NOT snail's eggs!'

'You would say that, wouldn't you? I'm a university professor and I know all about snails laying their eggs beneath the surface of the compost,' Steven continued.

'Maybe, Sir, but I got my degree in Horticulture at Bath university and my thesis was on plant pests and diseases. I can assure you that those plugs are fertilizer pellets,' Lauren replied, aware of the sniggering girl students watching them argue.

'Well, I suppose I'll just have to take your word for it then,' snapped Steven. 'Come on ladies, we'll go and get a coffee.' With that, the party headed off to the garden centre café.
Crossing from the car park into the yard, Lauren recognized Joy, Betty's daughter, with another nursery school helper, leading a small group of three and four year olds into the garden centre.
'Hello Lauren, we've come to choose some pretty flowering plants for our nursery garden, haven't we children?' smiled Joy.

'That's lovely,' replied Lauren. 'Miriam's working just over there with the bedding plants and I'm sure she'll be able to help you find something you all like.'

'We're growing our own sunflowers!' four year old Lucy said proudly, 'and I grew some marigolds!'

'Oh well done,' Lauren replied, as the group headed off to talk to Miriam.

Jeremy had seen the children enter the yard from his office window and came down to meet them, carrying two customer shopping baskets.

'Joy, put what plants you need in these baskets, for your nursery school,' he said,

'There's no charge. It's a gift from the Unicorn.'

'That's very kind of you, Sir,' Joy replied 'and very much appreciated. The children love their little garden.'

Jeremy smiled, as he watched Miriam and Joy showing the children which flowering plants would work best in their little garden. Then he suddenly remembered something.

'Lauren,' he began, 'Cornhaven village hall is hosting a Gardeners' Questions evening next week and I've been asked if we could provide someone to go on the panel. How would you feel about joining Tom, to answer gardeners' questions?'

'Never done anything like that before,' Lauren replied 'but I'm happy to give it a go , if Tom's there too.'

'I think the garden club will have two of their own members on the panel, too. And it's likely it will be recorded for a local radio broadcast. It could prove good publicity for the garden centre,' Jeremy continued.

'Then it's a 'yes,' said Lauren. 'Which

evening?'

'Actually it's Tuesday,' Jeremy replied, 'will that be OK?'

'Tuesday it is then. I'll see if Mark and I can get a baby-sitter for Oliver, so Mark can come too.'

Lauren knew that her weekend, apart from working part of Saturday, would mean a frantic searching through all her plants and pests reference books, to update her knowledge, ready for Tuesday evening.

The following Tuesday evening, Cornhaven village hall was buzzing with people. Lauren and Tom were led to their places on the stage by the village's well-known gardening brothers, Mike and Barry Enfield, who took their places on the stage next to Lauren. Microphones were clipped to their collars and a list of possible questions was placed in front of them.

Lauren noticed Jeremy stood at the back of the hall, talking to a tall, dark haired man who had a complicated sound recording system set in front of him. There was something familiar about the tall man, although Lauren couldn't quite place him.

Then she realized she was looking at Denzil Coombs! He was, or had been a regular presenter on the B.B.C. 'Spotlight' programme, watched every evening by her parents in Devon. Within minutes, Denzil was walking towards the stage, microphone in hand, ready to start the evenings proceedings.

Lauren and Tom were well supported in the hall, with most of the garden centre staff present, plus some of Miriam's fellow choristers from the parish church, along with their new vicar, Reverend Patricia Armstrong, who was sitting next to Lady Jane.

Denzil raised his hands for silence, signaling to a colleague to start recording.

'Good Evening, Everyone and welcome to Cornhaven village hall for tonight's 'Gardeners' Questions.' I'll start by introducing our four gardening experts on the panel.

We have two expert plants people from the Unicorn garden centre, Tom Waters and Lauren Harrison, plus Cornhaven's own gardening experts with over forty years' gardening experience each, Mike and Barry Enfield.'

The audience applauded, then Denzil continued, 'So without further ado, may we have the first question, please?'

Denzil handed over his microphone to a young, fair-haired lady in the audience, who had raised her hand.

'I'm Melanie and have recently moved here to live. I need some advice on suitable plants for a new hedge, as I've been told by my neighbor's that some plants suffer badly when the salt winds come further inland in the winter months.'

Denzil took the microphone back from Melanie, asking Lauren if she would like to comment.

'Certainly there are choices, depending on the height and density of hedge you want,' Lauren began.

'I'm happy to give you some names of shrubs which have some resistance to salt winds. You could use the evergreen Escallonia, which flowers through the summer months, Grisellinia, another good evergreen, or perhaps Tamarisk, a good coastal plant with feathery foliage and pink flowers in the summer, once established. I know that Eleagnus is used to good advantage in Cornwall and the Scilly Isles, another strong evergreen which can be trained into a dense hedge. If you have the time to visit the garden centre, I'll be happy to show you these plants. Tom, is there anything you might recommend?.'

'I think you've named the main ones, Lauren, but if more height is required, coastal pines make an excellent windbreak hedge, or you could mix and match a selection of these plants.'

Mike and Barry nodded in agreement and Mike added, 'We use rosemary, Senecio or Brachyglotis and hebes quite a lot when we create coastal gardens, too. They all produce flowers and are good if you only need a low hedge or edging to a garden plot.'

Denzil thanked them for their concise answers, adding, 'Much food for thought there, Melanie. I believe our second question concerns growing fruit trees?'

'Good evening, panel. My name is Ivan and for several years now our apple trees have produced little or no fruit. I prune them regularly, so what would you advise me to do?'

Lauren shuddered inwardly. Fruit tree care was her absolute 'bête noire', as customers rarely took advice on what to do. This time it was Barry who came to the rescue.

'Can you tell me, Ivan, about how and when you prune your trees?'

'Every winter, without fail. I cut all those new shoots hard back. Every spring the trees make another lot of new growth, but no flowers or fruit worth mentioning.'

'And have you ever carried out a summer prune on those new shoots?'

'No, of course not. I don't see why I should.'

'Well, I'm afraid if you want fruit the following year, it's vital to reduce the new shoots back by about a third, to a strong bud in June. Don't try and remove them altogether.

If you remove all the new shoots every winter, there will be no flowers or fruit because fruit tree wood needs to age for two years before it produces flower buds. The golden rule is to prune in winter for new shoots but summer prune for flowers and fruit the following year.'

'Thank-you, I'll try to remember to follow that advice,' replied Ivan, taking his seat.

There followed questions on weed control, which compost to buy for which job and creating your own garden compost, one of Tom's favourite topics, as it was one job he had been doing very successfully for many years. He made the point of saying that not every part of every plant could be composted.

It was important NOT to include the roots of perennial weeds such as dock plants and the dreaded couch grass in your compost heap, because these could continue growing when the compost was used as a mulch on the garden, as they probably would not fully rot down.

Also, avoid adding diseased leaves, especially from rose bushes, as the infection could carry over to infect new plants.

One member of the audience commented on how her tomato plants had suffered following using supposedly well-rotted manure from the local stables on her greenhouse borders. Any farm-yard or stable manure needed to be stacked and kept for at least a year before use, because it could be contaminated with pesticide or cleaning materials such as bleach from the yard.

Lauren was asked which, if any, newly introduced plants she could recommend and based her answer on the colourful displays in Miriam's baskets and pots, adding that it might not be a good idea to save seeds from any of these, because they were nursery-created hybrids and might not breed true the following year, but some of the tender perennials could safely be propagated by taking cuttings through the summer months and over-wintering them in a greenhouse or conservatory.

Then, right at the end, a smartly dressed lady raised her hand and Denzil handed her the microphone.

'I wish to aim my question at Lauren and Tom,' she began. 'I'm Celia and I've been trying for some time to locate a particular plant which would solve all my needs. A good evergreen with large clusters of either bright pink or purplish-red flowers, especially in winter, it rapidly covers bare walls, growing in poor soil and needing very little attention. I see it everywhere growing by the sea, but never for sale here; why?'

Tom said he could only think of the rhododendron family, but did not recognize the description of flamboyant flowers through the winter months.

'Are you quite sure it was in full flower in winter, Madam?' he asked.

'Yes, yes! And absolutely everywhere I went,' Celia answered.

Something clicked in Lauren's mind.

'Are you sure it was here, in this country, Celia,' she asked.

'Well no. It was probably Menorca. I spend my winters there. But that doesn't make any difference now we have 'global warming,' does it?'

'I'm sorry, I think it does,' Lauren replied. 'If you look in our houseplant department at the garden centre, you will see a selection of Bougainvillea plants. These are especially colourful as Christmas approaches and I know they grow tall in warmer, drier climates than ours. I think it will be many years before we can just leave them to grow outdoors unprotected all year round.'

With that, Denzil drew the Gardeners Questions evening to a close. The panel received rapturous applause and everyone agreed it was a great success.

Tom's wife, Susan, Jeremy, Miriam and Mark came forward to congratulate Tom and Lauren on their sensible answers.

The Enfield brothers asked them if they would be happy to do another session, perhaps in the autumn and Denzil Coombs, smiling, said he would be in touch to let them know when the programme was going out on local radio.

As there was still time, Jeremy suggested a drink at The Fisherman's Rest, before they all headed home, although Lauren decided it would have to be tea or coffee. Her head throbbed!

The Merry Month of May Continues.

Fortunately for Lauren, she had arranged to take the following day, Wednesday, as her day off work that week. The following weekend marked the last day of the Chelsea flower show in London, when both Piers and Lucas would be away and Lauren, along with student Clive would have the water garden department to look after, as well as all the plants.

Besides, Lauren needed to make arrangements with her parents in the South Hams to take Oliver for half-term week, because Mark's mother was working and Mark was unsure about having Oliver with him the whole of each working day. They would make the most of a day out together on the Sunday, when they travelled down to Modbury.

At the Unicorn garden centre, Miriam had an unusual 'find' in the old glasshouses. Jeremy met with her there, to check up on orders of planted hanging-baskets still awaiting collection or delivery.

'Come and see what I've found!' Miriam said excitedly. 'Look! Over there on the far bench near the door!'

Curled up, a tight bundle of reddish-brown hair, in an old crate was - - - a fox, fast asleep.

'Well I never!' Jeremy exclaimed, 'so that's what they look like!'

'I think it's been let loose by that woman down the road, you know, the one with the weird name? I've heard she saves foxes and other wild animals. A sort of sanctuary? I think her name's Tallulah.' Miriam said.

'Wasn't she one of your mother's friends?' Jeremy asked. Just then his phone buzzed. He was needed back at his office. 'Got to go, Miriam. Hope you're still OK to come out for dinner with me on Friday?

'Yes, definitely,' Miriam smiled as he left.

Alan had just finished fork-lifting several pallets of potting compost into the sales yard, where Malcolm had been busy helping customers with a whole range of the heavier goods; stone troughs, terracotta pots, paving, grit and compost.

They checked that Clive was free to take over the sales with one of the part-time staff and decided it was time for a coffee break.

Alan and his partner, Jenny, both had a keen life-time interest in anything paranormal, especially the UFO phenomenon, enjoying summer evenings sky-watching, when the weather permitted.

As they drank their coffee in the staff room, Alan was quizzing Malcolm as to whether he knew of any unusual activity in the skies over Cornhaven.

'Only thing I can think of is those flashes of white light, from time to time, seen over the forest at the back of Lady Jane's place. No-one I know feels threatened by them, though. Been there for many years, they say. Perhaps it's something electrical?' Malcolm queried.

'Jenny and I will be heading over to the Wiltshire downs soon,' Alan said. 'I'm waiting for reports of the first crop circles this year.'

'Thought all that was down to local lads with planks making patterns at night, though I've heard some turn up in a very short time in the dark. Would be interesting to know exactly how they do it, if it is just lads mucking about. How do they make those huge shapes in the crop? Anyway Alan, we've had our allotted time, so better get back to earning a crust, as they say. Got Alice here on work experience again today, so I'd better check that all's fine with her. She's helping Julie in the coffee shop.' With that, Malcolm rinsed out his coffee cup and the two of them returned to their respective jobs.

By now, Miriam had gone back to the garden plants area, happy to see several of her regular customers there, buying their bedding plants.
Lady Jane stood near the shop entrance, in conversation with another well-dressed woman, who Miriam recognized as Mrs. Dorothy Marshall, chairperson of the parish council.

As Miriam looked up from her work sorting through the plants, she heard Lady Jane exclaim, 'Who on Earth is THAT?!!'
Crossing the yard, walking towards the shop, she saw an ageing figure wearing bright purple and green tie-dyed clothing, her long, grey hair loosely plaited, leading a child, a boy of perhaps four years, with bare feet and equally bright clothing, by the hand.

Tallulah Beaconsfeld had arrived. Miriam hoped she hadn't come to look for the fox cub sleeping peacefully in the old glasshouse.

'I don't know WHAT this place is coming to!' Lady Jane stated stiffly to her friend; 'Tie-dyed clothing, bare feet and lady vicars! It's just not right for Cornhaven. Might as well be living in TOTNES!'

'But our lady vicar's really nice,' said Dorothy.
'Oh I know THAT,' replied Lady Jane, 'I spent yesterday evening sitting next to her, but it's not truly BRITISH, is it? Not part of our traditions.

'Oh well, just have to accept things as they are, I suppose.'
With that, the pair of them headed off to the

garden centre coffee shop, to annoy Julie and her crew of helpers.

The coffee shop was beginning to fill up with the 'ladies who lunch' brigade, mainly from the village. Lady Jane and Dorothy Marshall selected a table overlooking part of the outdoor sales area and young Alice bravely came over to take their order, luckily just for coffee and cakes.

Manager Julie was trying out a new idea of proper table service, with a selection of cakes being taken to customers to choose exactly what they wanted. Alice proudly carried the cake-stand to Lady Jane's table, while Julie brought over the coffees.

'Nice to see you here working today, Alice,' began Lady Jane, 'my friend and I will each have a slice of the coffee and walnut cake, please.'
Alice managed to serve the cake neatly with tongs onto two pretty floral china plates, then carefully carried the cake stand back to the kitchen.

'I think that young girl is amazing,' said Dorothy, 'and good on you for employing someone with Downs' syndrome, too.'

'I think we just have her here one day a week at the moment, on work experience,' Lady Jane replied, 'but she shows a lot of promise. Julie has said she would be willing to take Alice on full time, when she leaves school.'

Just then there was a commotion on the far side of the room. An elderly gentleman sitting at one of the tables had collapsed onto the floor. His wife, bending over him, called out for help.
Shirley, who was trained in first aid, came out from behind the counter to see to him and immediately shouted to Julie to call for an ambulance. Shirley was convinced the man had

suffered a heart attack. What was worse, there was now a queue of people waiting for a table and when the paramedics finally arrived, they struggled to get to their patient, who showed no sign of recovery. Julie tried her best, with her staff, to keep people back and allow the poor man and his wife some space.

As they had failed to bring him round, the paramedics maneuvered their patient onto a stretcher and took him out to the ambulance, followed by his wife.

Before the coffee shop staff had a chance to properly clear and clean-up the table, one pushy woman forced her way through shouting, 'The table's mine!' sitting down, grabbing a menu.

'Well, I've never seen anything like that before,' said Dorothy.

'Poor man, perhaps he died.' She was right - he did.

Miriam, surrounded by customers in the yard, watched the paramedics carry the stretcher out to the ambulance and drive off, bound for Southampton hospital. Tallulah, standing nearby, said she was sure that the couple involved had recently visited her native wildlife sanctuary.

The little lad with Tallulah was her youngest grandson, Zorro (his mother's choice, apparently) After quizzing Miriam on the present whereabouts of her parents, especially her mother and not getting a direct answer, Tallulah said that she hoped to encourage Zorro to have a go at growing vegetables and had come to get some ideas on which ones would be best for beginners.

She herself grew a wide range of herbs (Ahem!) but actual vegetable growing was not really her thing. Zorro's nursery school had closed for half-term, so it was up to Granny Tallulah to take care of him while his mother was working at the local stables.

Miriam helped them select some young vegetables in packs of ten; carrots, lettuce, peas and cabbage, then left them looking through the rack of vegetable seeds in the shop. Miriam found them a beginners' guide to vegetable growing book, as well. She knew that despite appearances to the contrary, Tallulah was not short of money.

By the time Friday evening arrived, Miriam was a nervous wreck. She had gone through her limited wardrobe several times, trying to decide what to wear, for her dinner date with Jeremy, finally settling on a simple, pink on purple, floral print dress and her favourite dusky pink summer jacket, in the hope that she would not need a raincoat, as the weather had been a bit unsettled that week.

While searching through her clothes, she had inadvertently opened a box in a drawer in the bedroom and out fell the engagement ring that David had given her twenty years ago, plus a photo of the two of them with Joanne, at five years old, on the beach at Barton-on-Sea. They were such happy, simple times, back then.

Was she being disloyal to David's memory by feeling attracted to Jeremy? She had lived without a husband for almost six years and now Joanne was making her own way in the world, there were times when loneliness really got to Miriam. Yes, there were friendships with people her own age, of both sexes, but there had never been anyone else for her since David died.

She knew both Joanne and her own mother

would just say, 'Go for it! Life's for living!,' but something was holding her back.

By the time Jeremy's car drew up outside her cottage at 7pm sharp, Miriam's mood had brightened and she greeted him with a smile on her face.

Jeremy, dressed smartly casual in grey linen jacket and trousers with a pale blue, open necked shirt, complimented her on her appearance, as she sat beside him in his car.

'So, where are we going?' Miriam asked.

'A friend from Oxford, Richard Perriment, has opened his first restaurant in Bournemouth,' Jeremy replied. 'He's named it 'Riches,' trying to be on the gourmet side, I think. It's right in the town centre, so he should do well.'

Jeremy drove carefully along the busy roads into Bournemouth. After finding a parking space in the main car park, between the town centre and the sea front, the couple headed towards the shopping centre to find 'Riches,' which turned out to be just on the winter gardens side of the town and had a black and gold painted exterior, with large, plate glass windows and huge potted plants.

'This looks rather expensive. I hope I can understand the menu,' remarked Miriam.

'Well, I've studied French, Latin and Greek, in the past, so we'll work it out between us!' Jeremy laughed.

They were warmly greeted by Richard himself and shown to a table for two, overlooking the park.

Jeremy smiled as he saw Miriam's eyes light up, as she read the menu. No foreign words on this one.

'Wow! It all looks good,' she said. 'I really

don't know what to go for.'

'Well, let's start with a glass of wine each, while we decide,' replied Jeremy.

In the end, they both chose a cheese soufflé starter, followed by oven roasted duck breast for Miriam and a medium fillet steak for Jeremy.

The food was very well presented, with a good selection of vegetables, too. When it came to the dessert menu, Miriam settled for a simple lemon sorbet, whilst Jeremy enjoyed a generous dish of Eton Mess (well, what else!)

They took their time over coffee to discuss how good the food was and to let Richard know they would love to return.

Afterwards, as the weather was still being kind, Jeremy suggested a walk to settle their meal.

Before entering the park, they passed by a jewelers, closed now, no gems in the windows, but there was a poster showing engagement and dress rings, which caught Miriam's eye and for a moment her mind drifted back to David and the ring he had bought her in Lymington.

'Penny for them, Miriam,' Jeremy had noticed her change of mood. 'Did you come here with your late husband?'

'No, he preferred shopping in Lymington or New Milton,' she replied, 'but Joanne likes Bournemouth and we often shop here, when she's at home.'

They walked on into the park, through displays of wallflowers, bellis daisies and tulips, soon to be replaced by summer flowering bedding plants.

It was getting dark as they neared the sea front and pier. The tide was in, with the waves lapping gently on the sandy shore.

'I love the sound of the sea. Usually I'll go

for walks along the cliffs at Barton-on-Sea, through the golf course to Milford, but this part of the coast makes me happy, too,' Miriam smiled.

'Good. Look, the amusement arcade's still open, let's try our luck!' laughed Jeremy. On his third attempt at playing on a crane or grab machine, he hooked out a soft toy, a pink and white unicorn, which he presented to Miriam, with a flourish.

'Something to remind you of this evening, my lady!' he said.

'Well thank-you, kind sir, I'll cherish it forever,' Miriam giggled, bowing to him.

As the attendant was fussing around them with his vacuum cleaner, they decided it must be time to leave. After a short walk along the almost deserted sea front, they headed back up the hill to the car park.

Before getting into the car, Jeremy reached out to take Miriam's hand. 'I've really enjoyed being with you this evening, Miriam,' he began. 'Please say we can do this again sometime soon.'

'I'd love to,' Miriam replied, with sincerity.

'It may not be for a while,' Jeremy said, a little sadly, 'as I'm taking my mother to stay with her sister Cerys in North Wales next week, then I've got a trades association business conference to attend in the Midlands, so I won't be at home much for the next three weeks. But I'll be back by the last week in June.'

'I'll look forward to the last week in June,' Miriam smiled, her eyes sparkling.

Jeremy was keen not to rush into showing too much affection towards her, though he certainly felt it. He knew he would have to tread carefully, as the last thing he wanted was to drive her away altogether. So, he settled for a gentle kiss on her cheek, as they parted at her cottage gate.

Saturday morning found Lauren, Clive and Malcolm looking after the outdoor part of the garden centre, along with two Saturday lads. In addition, Lauren and Clive had to keep an eye on Piers and Lucas' water gardening department, including their indoor shop area.

Lauren's biggest worry as manager, was guarding against shop lifting, especially theft of the more valuable items, such as pond pumps, fountains, garden lighting and other electrical equipment for outdoors, so she spent some time showing student Clive what to look out for and made sure they took their breaks separately. Luckily, Betty was in as well, on the tills, with two of her shop staff. Nothing passed Betty's eagle eyes.

The morning passed without incident. Not too many telephone enquiries and good sales of plants and various sundries going through the tills. Then, around 3pm, Betty called Lauren over.

'I'm a bit worried about that lot,' she said, waving her hands towards two young women pushing baby buggies towards the back of the shop.

'I've been watching them going in and out of the water gardening area for about twenty minutes or so. Clive's asked them if they need any help and they've said 'no,' but why would they keep going back in?'

Just then, Clive came running up to them.

'Lauren, thank goodness you're here!' he said.

'I think two pond pumps have gone missing!'

Lauren wasn't sure whether the customers had heard him or not, but they seemed to have disappeared. Seeing the women with the buggies crossing the yard, she ran out after them, closely followed by Clive.

Suddenly, realizing they were being followed, reaching into the buggies, the women jettisoned two boxes onto one of the shrub benches, as they headed for the car park. Fortunately the pumps were still in the boxes.

'What do we do now?' asked Clive, 'should we have challenged those women?'

'No. Not this time,' Lauren replied. 'They'd only deny it; but at least we know what they both look like, if they turn up again, plus Jeremy can check the security camera footage later. Thankfully we've got those pond pumps back.'

She was relieved that Piers and Lucas' department had not suffered any losses and hoped they were enjoying their time at the Chelsea flower show.

Malcolm was walking across the yard towards her.

'Lauren, I made a note of the number plates on the vehicles used by those women. Guess what? One of them got into that green van that Alice noticed the other day. Writing on the side says 'Grey's Green Gardens.' Looks like a landscape set-up to me. Wonder if that was who nicked the rockery stone and white chippings the other day?'

'Right, best pass this information onto Jeremy, when he comes in,' replied Lauren. 'At least we know who to look out for. By the way, Malc., do you know what they would use the white chippings for? I've only ever seen them on graves.'

'It's the tarmacking brigade,' Malcolm answered. 'Folks seem to prefer white chippings added to their newly tarmacked driveways to make them look more upmarket or something, plus giving added grip for wheels. Miriam not in today?'

'No, it's her Saturday off, but I think she's busy helping Tom plant some tubs outside Lymington town hall,' Lauren replied.

'What do you reckon to her and our Jeremy, then?' grinned Malcolm

'I know she likes him, but I don't think it's more than that. Anyway, they're both free and single, so it doesn't matter, does it?'

Lauren took the information Malcolm had given her into the shop, so that Betty could add it to her account of the afternoon's events, in the 'incident' book.

Just enough time for a quick check through Miriam's houseplant department, to make sure they had sufficient water and would keep until Monday morning, then it would be time to lock up, checking that any messages for Jeremy or Lady Jane were left in their offices.

On Sunday morning, Lauren and Mark helped Oliver pack his case for his half-term week away with his grandparents at their Devon home. They planned to leave early enough to make it to Modbury in good time for a 1pm lunch. Lauren's parents had a table booked at one of the local pubs, famous for its Sunday carvery meals.

The sun shone, as they drove down from Hampshire, through part of Dorset, into Devon, getting to Totnes around mid-day and enjoying seeing all the different wild flowers and fresh, green hedges, as they headed towards Modbury. The South Hams certainly had a lot to offer in early summer.

Lauren's parents still lived in her old family home, set in the hillside, about a mile from Modbury centre. Her mother, Hazel Hansworthy, was quite well known locally as an artist, selling her landscape paintings in several galleries and gift shops throughout the South Hams. Lauren's father, Roger, retired from the police, kept himself busy with a whole load of hobbies, when he wasn't needed to help out with repairs on one of the local estates.

Oliver especially enjoyed helping Granddad with his model railway, housed in a huge, lined shed in the back garden.

When the weather was good, they would drive down the narrow lanes to spend time on the beach at Bigbury-on-Sea, enjoying the walk at low tide across to Burgh Island, made famous by Agatha Christie.

Arriving in Modbury in good time for lunch, the family all met up in the town car park and walked to the carvery together.

Lauren's parents were very excited about her part in the Gardeners Questions radio show, which, as it turned out, was the same one broadcast in their area too.

'Fancy you meeting that Denzil Coombs!' her mother exclaimed, 'could make you famous yet!' They were all looking forward to hearing the programme being broadcast on the following Tuesday evening, repeated on the Sunday morning.

After a very enjoyable, well-cooked Sunday lunch, they took Oliver's holiday case to his grandparents' house for the week ahead. Lauren and Mark were in no great hurry to do the two and a half hour drive back to Romsey, so they all decided to visit a local garden,

Mothercombe House, open to raise money for charity. Lauren was especially interested because they also sold plants and she liked to see what they were charging.

Another of her favourite places to visit in the area was Avon Mill garden centre, run along similar lines to the Unicorn, but smaller and a favourite stop-over for walkers, as they had a good café, but there would not be enough time to do both that afternoon.

Mothercombe did not disappoint, with its tall echiums which had survived the mild winter, looking good to be fully flowering within the month, plus early roses, lavenders and many shrubs and perennials showing lush new growth and some flowers.

A local nursery provided the plants for the sales area, which included old-fashioned roses. Lauren thought the prices were fair for that area.

They decided to do the walk down to a sheltered, rocky beach, where they rested for a while, just enjoying the scenery.

'There are times,' began Lauren, 'when I really miss living down here.' She was watching Oliver, playing at skimming stones with his Dad and Granddad.

Her mother looked up and said, 'I know, Lauren, but you've just got to make the best of what you have got in this life and it sounds as though both you and Mark are enjoying your work. We all have our ups and downs and you know your Dad and I will always be glad to help where we can, especially with Oliver. He's such a lovely lad.'

'I'm so grateful you can take him this week. 'I've got an event to go to on Tuesday, then my boss is away and Mark's regular clients need him this week too. Should get the following

Saturday off, though, as long as the others can cope with my department. Got to admit I am enjoying the new challenge. I've certainly met some interesting people,' Lauren smiled to herself.

They walked slowly back up the lane to Mothercombe house for a cup of tea, before leaving.

Joyous   June

The end of May, slipping into June, brought settled weather and continued good sales for the Unicorn. Jeremy called his usual Monday morning meeting, to inform his staff just how well things were going, but stressed his concern over the shop-lifting attempts.

The women who had tried to take the pond pumps had apparently tried the same thing at another water garden centre some miles away, near Southampton and were known to the police.

There was no evidence to link them to any other theft, including stealing rockery stone, which Jeremy thought MUST be less likely, now he had the new security system up and running.

'But please,' he began, 'keep very vigilant and make notes on anything and anyone unusual, especially during my absence over the next two or three weeks. Tomorrow Lauren and Clive will be going to an event in Sussex, so please make sure there is someone on duty all the time, to watch both the shop and outdoor sales areas.

Jed will be in charge of any financial matters, as well as taking messages for both my mother and myself. Thank-you, everyone.'

Both Lucas and Piers were keen to speak to Lauren about their visit to the Chelsea flower show, the previous weekend. Lucas was enthusiastic about his water garden design for the following year, including Lauren's recommended plants and both of them felt inspired by what they had seen at the show.

It now looked very likely that the planned show garden would go ahead. Lauren made a mental
note to ensure the required plants would be

reserved at their supplier's nurseries for the following May.

Lucas and Piers had already set aside some space, with Miriam's approval, to store the stone and electrical equipment needed in part of the old glasshouses, first checking that the area would remain dry. Any wiring needed would have to be kept inside the shop, just in case it was disturbed by the sand lizards!

It turned out to be a busy Monday. Miriam's customers called in to collect the last of the pre=booked summer hanging baskets, plus she had a delivery of beautiful orchids from Burnham nurseries in Devon to find room for, displaying some of them near the shop tills, with Betty's permission, of course! Lauren found that she needed to place a further order for bedding plants, to top up the spaces following Saturday's excellent sales.

Piers received a delivery of pre-formed garden ponds in the yard and was working on where to display them to best advantage.

Lucas had no less than three designs to work on, for customers wanting to improve or update existing schemes.

Betty declared the whole shop floor to be 'in a right mess,' and delegated various members of her staff to clean and sort through the shop displays.

Jeremy did employ a cleaner for the offices and staff areas, but preferred his staff to be responsible for the maintenance of the sales areas.

By lunchtime, life at the Unicorn was less hectic. Miriam was quite excited because a reporter from the local Cornhaven Gazette had turned up while she was working with Tom, planting up tubs outside Lymington town hall and insisted on taking a photo of the two of them with the mayor, who was delighted with the regular planting they did, to improve the front of the building.

Miriam was looking forward to seeing her photo in the following Friday's edition. There would also be a mention in the reporter's article about all the plants used coming from the Unicorn garden centre, where she was a supervisor.

'There you go, Miriam, fame at last!' Lauren smiled. 'What with that and the radio broadcast tomorrow evening, I think we're now well and truly 'on the map!'

During the afternoon, Jeremy called Lauren and Clive up to his office, to discuss their visit to Sussex the next day, to the nurseries Lauren always called 'the Sussex group.'

'In fact,' Jeremy began, 'you will see work going on at a total of four nurseries. It's a full-on day and I would like you both to take notes, especially on new, upcoming varieties of plants. Lauren, feel free to take our smaller van, if you would rather use it than your own car, for insurance purposes. I have been sent a brief itinery for the day.

I did this tour with Tom two years ago myself, so I know it's very worthwhile. You only have to drive to the main centre at Littlehampton, then you will meet up with other delegates and be taken by coach to their various sites. Lunch will be provided, a rather good one, if I remember correctly!'

'Goodness, it's further away than I thought,' Lauren commented. 'But that's fine. We'll just have to make sure we leave here in good time tomorrow.'

'I suggest by 8.45am, to make sure you are in Littlehampton for the 10.30am start,' replied Jeremy.

'Good luck. I'm sure you'll enjoy the day.'

Lauren arrived at the Unicorn garden centre to collect Clive, shortly after 8.30am the following morning. Both of them were in their garden centre uniforms with Lauren sporting her plant area manager's badge.

After checking that the van had sufficient fuel, they left the garden centre a little before 8.45am, bound for Cadnam, where they would join the M27 motorway, heading out along the south coast to Littlehampton.

Lauren was used to driving long distances in her previous work, but today there seemed endless hold ups with heavy traffic and road works. It was almost 10.30am when they arrived at the main nursery yard at Littlehampton for a welcome coffee break.

Meeting up with other delegates, altogether there were thirty-five visitors plus some nursery staff boarding two coaches, to head for the first nursery, Walberton nurseries.

On entering the nursery, they were shown the first of the late summer batches of Hidcote lavender plus the larger growing lavender Vera, which would be ready to buy in August. There was a special promotion coming up for summer sales, the lovely, blue flowered Caryopteris, one for Lauren's 'special plants' bench, once people had grown tired of buying annual bedding plants.

Clive admired some really good red and yellow forms of the strappy-leaved crocosmia, which the nursery had set aside as part of its plant breeding programme, although the red flowered variety was expected to be sold in limited numbers the following year.

Lauren said she was very impressed with both the quality of the plants and the cleanliness of the whole, large nursery. Not a weed in sight! They were told that two men were employed full time to keep the nursery free of both weeds and pests.

With the sun full out, the weather was getting really hot. They were taken through the 'fogging house,' which was just like being in a sauna. Clive said what a shame there was no swimming pool outside! But it was worthwhile to see how cuttings were being taken and plants produced from shrubs growing on the nursery. Lauren remarked on the great attention to detail and the good care being taken of all the plants, right from the cutting stage through to the finished plant ready for sale.

At just before 12am, it was time to leave the Walberton nursery, travelling by coach to visit Starplants nurseries, a short drive away. This was a much smaller concern, but still showing the same attention to detail to both shrubs and climbers, which Lauren purchased regularly. Clive was impressed by the method of cutting back climbing plants in their pots in the early part of summer, to produce a quality plant for autumn sales.

'Gosh, I feel I have so much to learn, just on the wholesale side of the business,' he said to Lauren.

'Have you decided yet on which area you'd prefer to work in?' Lauren asked him.

'I thought, once I got my degree, I'd like to go into research, but I also enjoy the growing process,' he replied.

'I expect it will come down to what jobs are on offer at the time.'

'It's good to be flexible,' Lauren said. 'My husband just likes being his own boss.'

After they visited the dispatch department, it was time to leave for lunch at the Arundel Resort Hotel.

As Jeremy had hinted, the meal laid on for them certainly did not disappoint. The cold buffet was laid out on tables with eight place settings each. Waiting jugs of iced water were very welcome indeed, as the day was exceptionally warm for early June.

The wine was served and everyone settled down to a very enjoyable lunch, with fresh fruit salad for dessert, followed by coffee and delicious white Belgian chocolate.

The whole party were just a little late leaving for Binsted nursery to see their herbs and alpines.

Once again there was a very warm welcome and lots of very healthy plants in spotlessly clean surroundings. Lauren was interested to see that there were trials being carried out on using different compost mixes, with peat reduction being an important concern.

The nursery manager was keen to get opinions on plants for the following year. They were thinking of a 'three colour' promotion, using various forms of dwarf campanula and diascia, which would give red, white and blue. Had that idea been overdone with the Jubilee celebrations?

Then it was time to move on to the final nursery on the list.

A thirty minute drive through the beautiful Sussex countryside, over the Sussex Downs, with deer and sheep grazing in the fields, brought the party to New Place nurseries.

Everyone was warmly welcomed and taken on a long but worthwhile walk to see fruit tree production, which included varieties such as Ballerina, Charlotte and Flamenco grafted apple trees, alongside row upon row of magnificent ornamental trees and healthy shrubs, including good specimens of Mohave Silver pyracantha.

There were whole fields of rootstocks where no fewer than one hundred thousand grafts would be carried out that year, everything home-grown, not imported.

New Place nurseries aim and specialty was the production of a shorter, bushier ornamental tree, to fit in the average family car. Back at their dispatch department, everyone met up once again for refreshments and a final chat.

The ice-cold orange juice, lemonade and cola, served with freshly sliced cake and biscuits were a perfect finish to a wonderful, informative, full-on day for the horticulturists. Geoff from Farplants, the main dispatch centre offered thanks to all the nurseries involved, on the visitors behalf, before everyone climbed back onto the coaches for the return journey.

It was almost 5.30pm, by the time Lauren and Clive got into the van for their return trip to the Unicorn. Although both hot and tired, they decided it had been a very worthwhile day out. Clive, in particular, said he had found it inspirational, when considering his future career. Lauren had taken loads of notes.

It was close to 7pm, by the time Lauren and Clive arrived back at the Unicorn, swapping the company van for their two cars in the main car park, as the garden centre gates were locked by now.

Jeremy had walked down the drive from Cornhaven Manor house with Hector, Lady

Jane's golden Labrador, to welcome them back and was glad to learn their trip had been worthwhile.

'I'm off to Wales tomorrow morning,' he told them,

'taking my mother to stay with her sister for a couple of weeks. Jed will be in touch with us both by phone, if any serious problems arise. I've also arranged to go on to visit some of our suppliers, plus I have a business conference to attend in Birmingham later this month, so I will be relying on everyone here to look after the place while I'm away. Hector's going to Wales too, this time. He's always well behaved on my aunt's sheep farm. Tom and Susan will be looking after the house here. So, I'll see you in a couple of weeks' time.'

'We'll be fine, Jeremy,' Lauren replied. 'Enjoy your time away.'

With that, the three of them left for their homes, arriving in good time to hear the Gardeners Questions' broadcast on their radios.

The next morning, Jeremy helped his mother pack everything she needed for a couple of weeks in Wales, plus Hector's requisites and his own case. With the larger of the two vehicles they owned fully loaded, Hector in his separate space in the back, Jeremy and Lady Jane set off for her sister and brother-in-law's farm.

It would take around three hours to drive there from Cornhaven and Jeremy had allowed for a couple of stops for refreshments, if needed, as it was turning out to be an exceptionally warm day for early June.

They arrived just after mid-day, to be greeted by a cheery Cerys Williams, along with her husband, Bryn.

'Hello Jeremy, come on in, Janice (Lady Jane only allowed her sister to call her Janice!) and Hector too, good boy! Our dogs are out on the farm with the men working, at the moment, so come on in and make yourselves at home.'

Cerys had prepared lunch for them all and afterwards Jeremy decided to take Hector out for a long walk. He loved the Welsh countryside.

'Now then, Janice,' Cerys began, after they had finished clearing the table and washing up,

'how's things with our Jeremy? I heard all about that Caroline in New Zealand. Does he have a girlfriend now?'

'Not one worth mentioning,' Lady Jane (Janice) replied, 'in fact, it's worrying me.'

'What's up?' her sister asked.

'He's taken up with one of the staff. Nice enough girl, young widow with a daughter at university, but not someone I would have chosen for him, at all. No breeding!' Lady Jane almost snapped. 'What's worse, he won't discuss it with me at all.

I only found out he'd taken her out because Jed told me. You may have met her when you last came down. Her name's Miriam.

Cerys was smiling to herself. She indeed remembered Miriam; very helpful, kind, pretty and gentle, but nothing 'upper' about her at all.

'I do remember Miriam and I thought what a lovely young woman she was, when I met her last summer,' Cerys replied. 'Look, Janice, after what happened with Caroline, you've got to be more open-minded about Jeremy's choice of girlfriend. I think he could do a lot worse for himself.'

'You don't see Miriam as a gold-digger then?' Lady Jane asked.

'No, in fact if you took the trouble to read

your local paper, which I did when I was staying with you, you would have read that it was Miriam's father who had that huge lottery win over a year ago. If Jeremy has finally found love, that relationship definitely needs encouragement.'

'Well, I never knew that. I'm surprised Jed did not tell me,' Lady Jane replied.

'That's one individual I'd NEVER trust. Might be fine with the books, but I think he can twist information to suit his own ends. How old is Jed now, anyway?'
Cerys questioned.

'92, but he insists he's still fit to work, so I tend to keep him on because Terrance rated him. Perhaps he really ought to go,' Lady Jane mused.

By this time, Jeremy had returned with Hector and was talking to Bryn in the yard outside the farmhouse. Jeremy planned to give himself a couple of days at the farm, before moving on to visit his various suppliers finishing up at the business conference.

At least the weather was looking good, possibly for the rest of June, though it was pretty warm for driving. Jeremy would be extremely grateful that his vehicle had air-conditioning. He would be back at the farm on the 19th June, to collect his mother and Hector for the homeward run.

Back at the garden centre, Miriam planned to have a major clean-up of the old glasshouses, now that the hanging-baskets were sold, to help time pass until Jeremy returned, but for now she would be busy taking care of Lauren's department, as well as her own, over the weekend.

Lauren intended making the most of having a free weekend, going back down to Modbury with Mark on the Saturday, staying overnight at her parents' house, before returning home with Oliver on the Sunday evening.

Lucas would be running the water garden department on his own on Saturday, because Piers was crewing for his sister and her husband on their yacht, moored in Lymington, planning to sail across to Yarmouth on the Isle of Wight.

Alan said he was happy to cover the yard area with the Saturday staff that weekend, as Malcolm wanted the day off.

Alan and his partner, Jenny had spent a couple of weekdays in the Wiltshire hills, trying to photograph early crop circles in fields of golden flowered rape seed, though the sudden high temperature spoiled the sharpness of the designs as the crop was growing fast.

Betty spent Friday making sure her two full-time shop staff were up to speed and could manage a whole day without her supervision, although at least Miriam would be on call if there was a problem.

Jed was in his element. With both bosses away, he saw himself as 'the man in charge.' He knew better than to interfere with the work the others were doing, but thoroughly enjoyed wandering between the three upstairs offices, checking through files and when he felt up to it, scrutinizing every corner of the various buildings with his notebook, looking for possible breaches of health and safety.

Julie in the coffee shop was wise to his ways and well-versed in buttering him up, offering the odd free cup of tea and pastries which 'have to be used today.'

The exceptionally good June weather meant a slump in sales, because people were more inclined to head for the beach, rather than go shopping.

Miriam and her assistant, Clare, spent pretty well all of Saturday watering plants to keep them alive in the drying heat.

Alan and Miriam were on locking-up duties, after first checking that Jed had left the offices, at the end of the day. Miriam decided she would have to find the time on Sunday to check the plants for water again, as it was so hot, but first of all she was committed to chorister duties for morning service in Cornhaven parish church.

She missed Joanne on Sunday mornings. When Joanne was home, they sang together in the choir. Tom and Susan were regular church members too and they all enjoyed meeting up for coffee and cake in the church hall, after the service. Tom had recently taken up the position of churchwarden and Susan liked to help Miriam with the flowers, one of a team of six ladies who kept the little church looking pretty, warm and welcoming.

That particular Sunday, as they sat with their coffees in the church hall, Tom and Susan were keen to hear how Joanne was getting on at university.

'What did you say her degree is in?' asked Susan.

'Anthropology, but she has a keen interest in archaeology too, and is going on a dig for the first part of the summer holidays. I do miss her company,' Miriam replied, wistfully.

'You know, Cornhaven is supposed to have an interesting past,' Tom said thoughtfully. 'Has Joanne ever looked into it? They say the name came about because many years ago it was a corn or wheat and barley growing area on the banks of a river, long since dried up, which linked across to the Beaulieu river and farmers used to transport their grain by boat all the way to flour mills in Southampton. So this place was the 'haven for corn.'

'I've never heard that one,' said Miriam, 'but perhaps Joanne would know. Never mind, we can ask her when she's home again in August. My parents should be back from their travels by then, too.'

Later, after she had checked the garden centre plants for water and cooked herself some dinner, Miriam decided to drive down to Barton-on-Sea cliff-top road, parking in one of the free roadside spaces near the café, so that she could go for a walk along the top to the golf course.

The roads between the forest and the coast were always busy, especially on Sunday afternoons, but it was good to see families having fun in the warm June sunshine.

She thought walking might just take her mind off Jeremy, for a while, but, if anything, it seemed to make her long for his company all the more. She felt that he wanted to know her better, too, but would his mother put a freeze on their relationship?

Miriam loved just being by the sea and decided to take the wide pathway leading down to the beach, from the café. It was such a joy to see the sun sparkling on the water, as the waves sucked at the sand and shingle. Today there was a lovely clear view across to the Isle of Wight and the Needles. She wondered if Piers and his relatives had managed to sail across safely to Yarmouth and back to

Lymington.

Her day-dreams were interrupted by the sound of loud voices on the lower path, close to a sandy part of the beach. Miriam saw it was a group of students enjoying a sort-of picnic and certainly recognized one of them - Clive! He had his arm round a pretty, blonde haired girl. Miriam thought she would just turn and walk on, but Clive spotted her and called her down to meet his friends, six of them altogether.

'Gorgeous day, Miriam. Would you like a
sausage roll?' Clive called out.

'We're celebrating the last week of exams, well, for some of us!'

He introduced her to his friends, some of whom knew Joanne, saying they hoped to meet up with her again in August. Miriam stayed with the students for a while, before making her excuses and heading back up the cliff path. The meeting had certainly lifted her spirits.

Monday morning found most of the staff sharing news about their weekends' activities around Betty's till area, before the 9am opening time.

Piers had a successful trip on his sister's yacht to Yarmouth and back and was keen to do it all again, later in the summer.

Lauren enjoyed her family time in the South Hams. On the Sunday morning they enjoyed the warm weather on Bigbury beach. At low tide, Oliver found hermit crabs in the rock pools on the edge of Burgh island and they all enjoyed a walk up to the highest point.

Malcolm, Jill and Alice had a picnic in their favourite part of the New Forest, where Alice was able to delight in watching new baby foals playing alongside their mothers.

Betty herself, however, was less chatty than usual. Miriam asked if anything was wrong and she replied that Joe, her husband, was worried about his job, working as an engineer in the railway sheds at Eastleigh.

'The trouble is,' she began, 'they are talking about reducing the staff there and as he's approaching fifty, he thinks he could be one of the first to go. Joe's even suggesting moving back to Cornwall, which I wouldn't want, as I enjoy my work here, plus our elder daughter, Joy's running the pre-school nursery and her sister's got another year yet with her business course at Southampton university.'

'We'd hate to see you go,' Lauren said. 'I really appreciate all the help you've given me, since I joined the company.'

'I'd certainly miss you,' Miriam added. 'I've learned so much from you over the last three years.'

'Well, let's hope Joe's worries come to nothing,' Betty replied. 'Right, you lot; time to unlock the gates and let the customers in.'

After a thorough check through houseplants and bedding plants, making sure they were all fit to sell, Miriam discussed her plan to clean out the old glasshouses, now the hanging-baskets were all gone, with Lauren, who agreed that it was a good idea. After checking that Clive was happy to man the main plant area, Lauren went with Miriam to inspect the old glasshouses.
They were delighted to see the young fox back again, curled up asleep in his crate.

'So how long will he stay?' Lauren asked.

'Usually most of the day, if he's not disturbed,' Miriam replied. 'I don't think he does any harm.'

Sand lizards scurried around their feet. Lauren

declared it to be the Unicorn wild-life sanctuary, which made Miriam laugh.

Although some of the old wooden benches definitely needed a wood treatment, Lauren said it would be a bad idea at the present time, because of the heat.

'Don't stay in here, if you feel too hot yourself,' she instructed Miriam. 'Extreme heat through the glass could make you seriously ill.'

Lauren did a mini stocktake of the plant area most Monday mornings, before checking what plants were on offer to buy from her wholesalers, that week. This time, Saturday sales were a little bit down, probably due to the hot weather, so she just put together a small top-up order for Farplants nurseries, whose sales representative, Andy, would most likely telephone her later in the day, plus some potted bedding plants from a local grower.

Just after her morning break, Lauren was called into the shop by Betty. There was a customer with a problem. Lauren just knew it would be related to growing fruit.

'Ah, Lauren,' Betty began, 'Mr. Thompson's brought back a couple of gooseberry bushes he bought from us last year. He says they won't produce any fruit.'

Mr. Thompson held out a black plastic rubbish sack towards Lauren.

'This is the second time I've bought fruit bushes from you and they've been no good!' he said, in an irritated fashion.

Lauren looked into the bag and saw the remains of two small bushes, severely cut back, with just a few juvenile shoots starting to grow.

'I'm sorry sir,' she began, 'but I think they may have been over-pruned.'

'NO, definitely not. Look, it's in this fruit plant expert book,' Mr. T. continued. The page he was waving in front of her was giving instructions on how a gooseberry bush was pruned in its first year from a cutting, not as a two-year-old, ready to grow on to produce fruit.

'You have to let the new shoots from the previous year grow on, if you want them to flower and fruit,' Lauren continued. 'I'm afraid the expert article is misleading.'

'I should have been told that when I bought these plants,' Mr. T. said angrily, 'it's the garden centre's fault. If I'd been told, I might be seeing some fruit on the bushes this summer. I want a refund.'

Lauren replied, 'Look, instead of a refund, why not take two pot-grown gooseberry bushes from our fruit section. They are good, strong, two to three year old plants and may yet fruit this summer. At least come outside and see them.'

'Oh very well!' he snapped. 'But if this doesn't work, I definitely want my money back!'

Having finally satisfied Mr. Thompson's desire for revenge, as he happily accepted the two pot grown gooseberry bushes, Lauren took the polythene bag with the two sad, badly pruned plants around to Miriam for potting. She was convinced that growth would resume and next autumn they would have two saleable fruit bushes.

The next day, Betty was agitated once more.

'Have you seen this lot?' she asked Lauren. On the counter in front of them was a stack of forms.

'It's from Jed. He wants us to give him more detailed time sheets about everyone's working day! Honestly, as if we don't have enough to cope with, what with the customers needing help and keeping the stock looking good.'

Lauren sighed, 'They tried this where I worked before, but it's hard when everyone's working flat out to find time for the extra paperwork. Does this mean the Mole's into time and motion studies now?'

Jed had divided every form to show the work carried out every thirty minutes and wanted to know exactly where in the garden centre everyone was working, including detailed listing of breaks taken. Each form had an employee's name and the week's dates at the top.

'Well, we'll just do the best we can, at least until Jeremy returns,' Lauren said, taking the relevant named forms for the outdoor staff and Piers and Lucas' department.

Betty picked up the remainder for the shop and coffee shop, saying, 'Julie's not going to like this.'

Miriam thought perhaps they only need write 'shop' or 'yard' against each half hour slot. Lauren agreed at least it was worth a try.

Miriam had to abandon plans for a major sort-out in the old glasshouses, leaving the fox cub in peace, although even he had to move out, because of the heat.

Lauren was glad to have her help outside, because she had to plan advance autumn tree and shrub orders and check confirmation of Christmas tree orders, which felt a bit weird in the heat.

She engaged Alan's artistic help in putting together a display table for coreopsis 'Flying Saucers,' due in at the end of the month. Alan had a gift for model making and planned a sort-of 'moon landscape' with a model flying saucer made from two silver – painted plastic plates, dangling from an overhead bar, on a piece of fishing line. Lauren agreed that it certainly would attract attention.

Two weeks flew by, what with dealing with customers plus Jed's extra paperwork for all the staff.

Miriam had asked Tom if Jeremy was returning home before his business meeting in Birmingham. Tom was able to tell her that Jeremy had literally dropped in for one night to get a change of clothes, briefly seeing Susan and regular housekeeper Ruth, before leaving early the next morning for the Midlands.

He planned to collect his mother and Hector from Wales the following weekend to return home on mid-summer's eve, when he had a meeting with his consultant. Miriam just had to be patient.

Love.

On mid-summer's eve, Jeremy was feeling very happy. His meeting with Noric had gone well. Generally the business was doing well. He knew he had made the right decision backing Lauren's application to take over from Tom.

Her ability to both select the right plants to sell, displaying them to best advantage and negotiate with his suppliers for the best deal was definitely paying off, cancelling Lady Jane's initial doubts on his choice.

Then there was Miriam. She was delighted to be recognized as a supervisor and he had to admit he was very fond of her. Strangely, his mother seemed to have changed her mind about Miriam, so maybe he could get to know her better?

However, Jeremy sighed as he remembered Noric's words, saying he must look to the future to secure and protect all they had.

Such a shame Caroline never wanted a child. Jeremy's fortieth birthday would be in less than a year's time and he had no heir.

Many thoughts filled his head as he walked back through the estate woodlands towards Cornhaven Manor. Darkness descended, as the full moon went behind a cloud, but the night remained warm, very warm.

Miriam was restless. After work that day she prepared a cold supper for herself, which she barely ate, because it was still so hot outside. She had a cold shower and slipped into a thin blue cotton dress.

Looking out of her cottage window, she could see the woodlands at the back of Cornhaven Manor. The moon had gone behind the clouds, but there were those strange white lights over the trees.

Suddenly she decided she needed to go for a walk. Slipping on a pair of sandals, she headed out, closing the garden gate behind her and walked along the footpath towards the edge of the forest.

There was a stile in the fence on the edge of the estate, allowing villagers access to part of the land, acting as a short, safe route for walkers to the back of the garden centre.

Miriam climbed over the stile and made her way along the path, once more well-lit by the moon. There was a flash of white light over the trees and for a moment she was not sure exactly where she was; strange, she had taken this path many times and was not afraid.

A little further on, the path opened onto grassland, often used as a picnic area, joining with a further, graveled path leading to the private estate woodlands.

Miriam froze as she heard footsteps a little way ahead, on the estate path, coming towards her. Her fear melted into relief as she got a good view of the figure in the moonlight and recognized; Jeremy!

'Miriam?' he asked, 'what are you doing here?'

'I just needed a walk,' she said, 'but I'm glad it's you, as I was beginning to get nervous.'

As she took a step towards him, her foot caught in a tree root and she stumbled. Jeremy leapt forward to save her. As she fell into his arms, he became aware of the softness of her body and the sweet floral perfume in her hair.

Miriam, strongly aware of his arms around her, started to apologies. As their eyes met in the moonlight, she realized that he cared about her.

He kissed her tenderly on her forehead

seconds before their lips met in a passionate embrace.

Overhead, Miriam saw another flash of white light and briefly wondered if she was in a dream. Jeremy's caresses were becoming stronger and she found herself responding. So many nights had passed when her whole body ached for him.

'Darling Miriam, I want you so much. I love you. Say you'll be mine, please.' Jeremy whispered into her soft, scented hair.

It was as if they were being lifted up and transported to another realm. Jeremy was at first surprised by Miriam's response to his caresses, then delighted, knowing she wanted him as much as he wanted her.

Her hands loosened his clothing, as she sighed deeply and he knew tonight his body would satisfy this beautiful woman, needing little encouragement. She made no attempt to make fun of him, as Caroline had done.

His hands were stroking her lovely body beneath the thin cotton dress. She wore no underwear.

Soon they were lying together, bodies entwined, on a carpet of dried oak leaves and their own discarded clothing, with the moon shining overhead. Deep love and passion overwhelmed them both and as they cried out together, Miriam fainted.

Some hours later, Miriam woke up from a deep sleep. She was back in her own bed in her cottage, thinking she must have been dreaming.

The blue dress was folded neatly on her bedside chair, with several dried oak leaves stuck to it. Her canvas sandals, grass-stained, were on the floor.

Confused, she realized it was a work day and she had less than an hour to wash, dress and have her breakfast, before heading over to the garden centre.

Arriving at her work, she was met by Betty.

'Oh, Miriam,' Betty began, 'Jeremy's asked for you to go up to his office. What have you done now?'

'Nothing I can think of,' Miriam replied, smiling inwardly at her thoughts of the previous night.

Jeremy was standing by his office window, as Miriam entered the room. He carefully slid the lock across on the door behind her, leading her over to the leather sofa at the far side.

'After I saw you home, I was worried - - -' he started to say, but she reached up to kiss him and stop him apologizing.

He smiled at her. 'So, how do you feel this morning about making it official?' Then without waiting for her reply, he dropped down on one knee before her.

'Miriam, I love you more than life itself, will you marry me?'

There were tears in Miriam's eyes, as she said,

'Yes!'

'Then we have some urgent shopping to do!' Jeremy said, as he kissed her tenderly.

'What, right now? She queried.

'Yes, right now!', he said, reaching into the top drawer of his desk and taking out his wallet and car keys.

'Come, My Lady, the Bournemouth jeweller's awaits us.'

Jeremy's initial suspicion that there just might have been someone listening in the corridor was well-founded, as a certain old man of shriveled complexion was seen just outside his own office door, as the couple were leaving.

'Jed!' Jeremy shouted to him, 'I have urgent business to attend to in Bournemouth, so will you please take any telephone calls that come in for me, in the next couple of hours.'

'Very well, Sir. I'll see to it,' came the reply.

Betty and Malcolm, standing at the shop entrance, saw Jeremy's car head out to the main road, with Miriam sat beside him.

'Oh, dear, I wonder if something's wrong with Miriam?' Betty mused.

'And we never got our staff meeting with Jeremy this morning, either. You'd think he'd have a lot to discuss, after being away all that time.'

Malcolm replied that maybe it could be good news and nothing to worry about. Anyway, they would know soon enough. With that, he went back to work in the yard.

Miriam decided she would prefer an engagement ring that included sapphire, because she knew sapphire stood for so many good qualities; - faithfulness, sincerity, loyalty, happiness and peace in a relationship. Jeremy urged her not to look at the price, just choose the one she really wanted.

The jeweller brought out a tray of the most beautiful sapphire and diamond rings and Miriam selected one that reminded her of a flower, a central sapphire surrounded by tiny diamonds. It was a perfect fit, no adjustment needed.

'And would Sir be interested in viewing our selection of wedding bands?' the sales assistant enquired.

'Why not,' Jeremy replied. The couple decided on matching bands in eighteen carat gold, the same as Miriam's engagement ring, but these did need some re-sizing and would be ready in a week or so.

'No rush,' said Jeremy, 'as we still have arrangements to make.' Miriam's ring was paid for, and they left in high spirits.

Miriam could not stop gazing at the beautiful ring on her left hand.

'Last night was wonderful,' she said to Jeremy. 'you've brought me fully back to life. I never thought I would know such happiness again. I'm so proud to be your fiancée.'

'I thought I would never experience true love, but now I have and I want it to be forever, my darling Miriam. You more than deserve the very best I can give you. Now, do you think you're up for sharing our wonderful news with certain other people?'

'Any chance of a coffee break first?' Miriam smiled.

'Certainly, my love. Let's see if Riches is open for coffee. Richard can be the first to know,' Jeremy replied, as they headed for the restaurant.

Lady Jane had decided to give herself a couple of days away from the garden centre, after returning from her sister's farm and was sitting in the conservatory on the north side of Cornhaven Manor house, with Hector in his dog bed near the open door, when Jeremy and Miriam arrived. Lady Jane had an open copy of the Cornhaven Gazette in front of her, with the photo of Tom and Miriam with Lymington's mayor on the inside page.

'Miriam, what a lovely surprise,' Lady Jane gushed, worrying Miriam concerning what was coming next.

'Your photo in no less than three local papers, Cornhaven, Lymington and New Milton. Very well done to you and Tom.'

'Mother, Miriam and I have news of our own for you,' Jeremy began, showing his mother the beautiful ring newly placed on his fiancée's left hand. 'This wonderful woman has agreed to become my wife.'

Lady Jane was silent for a few seconds, then lifted her eyes to meet Miriam's.

'Congratulations, both of you. You certainly have my blessing.' She reached out her hand to Miriam, saying, 'I'm so happy to welcome you into the family, as my new daughter-in-law.'

Stunned, Miriam just smiled, squeezing Lady Jane's hand lightly.

Hector was watching them, wagging his tail. Miriam walked across to make a fuss of him, as he licked her hand.

Watching them, Jeremy leaned towards his mother and said one word, 'Jed?'

'Yes, Jed,' she replied. 'He couldn't wait to call me after you two headed out and then there's this business with all that extra paperwork he's put on the staff. I'm seriously thinking its high time he packed it all in,' Lady Jane confided in her son.

'O.K. but he's given good service over the years. I'll watch him over the next few weeks,' Jeremy replied, cheering up as Miriam walked back across the room to him.

'Oh, and Miriam,' Lady Jane began, 'I know you two have yet to make your own plans, but please think about having the wedding reception here at the manor. There's plenty of space for a large marquee on the front lawn, plus perhaps we could make use of all those empty outbuildings. How about your own parents? Are they around?'

'Last time I heard from them, they were in Morocco making the most of part of Dad's huge lottery win,' Miriam answered, 'But they will be back here in August, as will my daughter, Joanne.'

'Splendid! Perhaps we can have a get-together, once they all return. Now, I think you two have some explaining to do to the rest of the staff!' Lady Jane said, smiling.

Malcolm looked up, grinning, as he saw Jeremy walking across the yard with his arm around Miriam. She did not need to flash the lovely jewels on her hand to show their relationship was finally out in the open.

'Congratulations you two! Not before time,' Malcolm shouted, as other members of staff, including Clive, Lauren and Betty, joined in. Customers shopping in the yard must have wondered what on Earth was going on.

'Oh, wonderful! I was so worried about you, Miriam. I thought something dreadful had happened. Betty remarked. 'Well done, Jeremy, I think you two make a lovely couple.'

Jeremy and Miriam were stunned by just how happy everyone else was, at their announcement.

Lady Jane's suggestion of a party at the manor the following Friday evening, was met with delight by all except Jed, who in true 'Mole' fashion just seemed to want to hide away.

'My lovely fiancée and I will have a spot of lunch in the coffee shop, then we'll be back to work as normal,' Jeremy told the workers. 'Staff meeting 8.30am sharp tomorrow, everyone.'

Julie, Shirley and the two other coffee shop ladies added their congratulations, as they served the couple with sandwiches and coffee. They all offered to help Lady Jane with the engagement party.

For Miriam, the days passed by in a blur. She spent some time on the telephone to her parents and Joanne, who were both surprised and delighted to hear of her engagement, but very happy for her and just wanted to get back to Cornhaven to join in the celebrations.

The earliest they could make it would be the first week in August. Joanne was willing to cancel going on the archaeology dig, but Miriam said not to, because she knew just how much Joanne had been looking forward to it.

The Friday evening party was for invited guests only, basically garden centre staff, their close relatives, Richard from Bournemouth, who Jeremy had lined up to be his best man and Miriam's friends from the choir at Cornhaven church.

Lady Jane also invited the vicar, but she had a prior engagement, though she did send her congratulations and said she hoped when it came to planning the wedding, the couple would consider their parish church, even mentioning that the August bank holiday weekend was free! Jeremy asked Miriam if she thought this might be a possibility, and her reply was, 'Why not! What's the point in waiting? At least my family will be in Cornhaven through August and September.'

So, the couple booked an appointment with Reverend Patricia for the following Wednesday.

Lady Jane was grateful for all the help she received, organizing the engagement party at Cornhaven Manor. Her housekeeper, Ruth, Susan and the coffee shop ladies made sure there was a generous cold buffet laid out in the main reception room, plus drinks in the conservatory, for the thirty-five guests. Hector decided it was all too much for an old dog and slept in the kitchen, under the old oak table. All being well, in ten weeks' time, there would be another party at the manor, Jeremy and Miriam's wedding reception!

Reverend Patricia had a surprise for Jeremy, when the couple called in to discuss their marriage, the following Wednesday evening.

'I found something I thought you would be interested to see, when I was going through some of the old boxes in the vestry,' she said, holding out a child's picture, drawn and coloured in, most likely at Sunday school.

'I think this was drawn either to show the child's view of their home, or of Heaven,' the vicar continued. It was a neatly drawn, coloured picture showing a large house with out-buildings, trees and a path leading into the forest.

There was an open, grassy area beyond the trees, with animals which may have been deer or ponies grazing and right at the very top of the picture, against the sky, a large white horse, no, a horse with a single horn between its eyes, - a unicorn!

'Look at the child's name,' rev. Patricia said and in the bottom right-hand corner was written TERRY W-S.

'My father!' Jeremy exclaimed. 'He must have drawn this when he was a child, here, in the Sunday school, a very long time ago.'

'It's yours to take home, if you want it,' rev. Patricia said, 'but I'm curious as to why he would draw a unicorn. Did he have a vivid imagination?'

Jeremy had no answer to that one, but was pleased to accept the picture to take back to his mother.

August bank holiday Monday was the date set for the wedding and Jeremy agreed that he would be in church when the banns were read, especially as Miriam would be there anyway, in the choir. He thought he might just go back to giving bell-ringing a go, having packed it in when he took over running the garden centre. It would be good to do something in the community outside of work.

Miriam expressed some slight unease when it came to whether or not they wanted a reference to the blessing of children in their marriage, because she had been told by doctors that Joanne would most likely be her only child, but in the end they both decided to include the words. Jeremy, Miriam knew, wanted a child, even if it meant adoption.

The warm weather broke with a heavy thunderstorm the following Monday, flooding part of the garden centre yard.

Something grey and bedraggled was crying between the pallets of compost in the yard. Malcolm reached in and pulled out a sorry-looking wide-eyed grey kitten. He decided to take it to Miriam, in the old glasshouses, where she was busy planting up four baskets of trailing begonias for a late summer display at one of the local pubs. Luckily the fox cub had moved on.

Julie had cats of her own, but said she could not find room for another one, even though it was only a kitten, so Miriam decided to take it in, herself, as she lived the nearest to the Unicorn, and it might yet be claimed by its owner.

'I'll call him 'Willow.' Miriam giggled. 'You know, Pussy Willow, about right for the garden centre, I think!'

Willow was found a towel and a box, plus bowls and cat food from the pets' section, arranged by Betty. He seemed so happy just to stay in the glasshouses, that Miriam decided he would make
a good nursery cat, keeping mice away from the wild bird seed and other stored goods.
Everyone wanted to make a fuss of him. Betty put up a notice in the shop to say he'd been found, but he never was claimed.

It took several days to clear the yard of damage and debris, following the thunderstorm, but the weather soon settled down, with a further heat-wave forecast. Lauren was able to supply Mrs. Webb with her longed-for purple loosestrife, later than she had hoped, but still welcome.

Lauren had asked for time off to cover part of Oliver's school holidays, from the end of July until mid-August, but all three of her family would be in Cornhaven for the wedding on bank holiday Monday.

In the meantime, Alan had come up trumps with his 'flying saucers' display, showing off a later flowering variety of Corcopsis Flying Saucers to good advantage. It attracted a lot of attention. He had even managed to find some tiny model aliens to place between the plants and rocky landscape.

Farplants delivered a trolley-load of patio roses in flower, shades of red, pink, apricot, yellow and also white, which were selling rapidly.

Useful plants for replacing those that had suffered in the previous heat wave, along with some beautiful begonias in full flower.

With the success of the 'flying saucers' display in mind, Lauren asked Alan if he thought they could do something to entertain visiting children through the summer holidays.

They decided on constructing a 'flowerpot men' tableau, loosely based on the old children's television characters, but bigger, under part of the covered area in the yard.

Miriam and Jeremy divided their spare time between the manor and Miriam's cottage, where she would cook an evening meal for the two of them and they could discuss their future plans, although even when they spent time with Lady Jane at the manor, Jeremy would walk or drive Miriam home afterwards and enjoy a very intimate 'nightcap' before returning home.

Lady Jane was in her element, getting quotes from caterers and making sure the outbuildings, a small barn and disused stables, were scrubbed clean for use by the wedding guests. There would be live music, laid on in the barn, a bar in part of the stable block and the main reception with the wedding breakfast in a huge marquee on the front lawn.

There were toilets attached to both the stables and the barn, used back in the day when the estate employed over twenty staff, which fortunately just needed a good clean and were perfectly serviceable. Lady Jane decided it could be 'Ladies' in the barn and 'Gents' in the stables!

Miriam loved pastel colours and decided she would like cream, shell pink and mauve for her wedding. She saw a cream, lacy fitted dress in the window of the ladies' dress shop in New Milton, which also had a wedding section. Luckily Alan's partner Jenny worked there, and Jenny was very happy to help Miriam with her choice. Miriam's first wedding, to David, had been at New Milton parish church when she was only nineteen and she had worn a traditional long white gown. This time, in agreement with Jeremy, who also wanted less formality, she thought she would prefer cream, perhaps with a head-dress of artificial rose buds.

The bridesmaid's dress would just have to wait until Joanne came home at the beginning of August, but she hoped Joanne would be happy with shell pink satin.

July passed in a blur of making wedding arrangements, in the exceptionally hot weather. Mid-morning on the first Saturday in August, Joanne crashed in through the cottage door, shouting, 'I'm home, Mum! Wow! You look fabulous! Being about to marry Jeremy obviously suits you.'

'Glad to have you home, darling!' Miriam replied, hugging her daughter.

'So, have you thought anything about what happens to this place when you're lady of the manor?' Joanne enquired.

'Yes, it's all yours, Joanne. I would not want to sell the cottage because it holds too many happy memories,' Miriam smiled to her daughter.

Joanne was full of news about her time on the archaeological dig, success on her anthropology course and looking forward to the next two years at university. She was so grateful to her grandparents for paying for it all, so there would be no debts for her to settle up.

'When are they home?' she asked.

'Next week and not before time,' her mother replied. 'So much still to sort out, but I'm so grateful to Lady Jane for organizing the wedding reception. My dress is more or less sorted out, but I need you to come into the shop with me to choose yours. I'm hoping you'll like shell pink,' Miriam continued.

'Whatever, Mum, not bothered. Shall we go there this afternoon?' Joanne asked.

'Let me find you something for lunch, first, then we'll go and see Jenny in the dress shop,' Jenny was pleased to see them both and able to show Joanne her mother's choice, a simple A-line frock in pink satin with short, capped sleeves, the skirt dropping from a below-the bust seam, with a pink rosebud trim on the seam and V neckline.

'I'm happy with this, Mum,' Joanne said, trying on one in her size, 'but I don't think I'd wear it out with the gang!'

Jenny put the dress to one side for them and as they were about to leave the shop, Miriam met up with Alice and her Mum, Jill, going through the dress rails in the main part of the shop.

'I've got my outfit, Miriam,' Jill said, 'but we can't find anything to suit Alice.'

Joanne pulled her mother to one side, whispering in her ear.

'Joanne, that's brilliant! If you're sure you don't mind, then I'm happy with that,' Miriam grinned.

'Alice,' she began, 'I think you need to go to the other part of the shop with Joanne and Jenny to be measured, as I'd like BOTH my bridesmaids to wear the same style frock.'

Alice's eyes opened wide, 'I've never been a bridesmaid. Do you really want ME?' she asked.

'Definitely,' Miriam replied. 'Off you go. Jenny will sort you out.'

Jill looked totally bemused as she thanked Miriam for her kindness.

'It will be dress, hair and make-up at my cottage for us girls on 28th. Shall we say 10am? The wedding's at 2.30pm,' Miriam smiled at Jill.

'That's lovely. I'll see she's there on time,' Alice's mother replied.

As Lauren was now on holiday for at least another week, Miriam enlisted Joanne's help in just checking through all the plants each day, to make sure they were healthy and fit to sell. Her assistant, Clare, was pretty good, but it was a lot to take care of. Miriam was so pleased that Jeremy had taken on extra sales staff, otherwise they would never cope, as the summer holiday season had brought many extra visitors to the area. At least Lauren would be back at work before the bank holiday and when Miriam and Jeremy were away on honeymoon.

The next day, Sunday, Joanne spent renewing old friendships in Cornhaven, starting with being back in the church choir with her mother. Everyone was delighted to see her and made her throat dry from answering endless questions about the university and her work.

Tom asked her if she had carried out any anthropological research on Cornhaven. Joanne replied that she had tried, but all she could find was a reference to someone being burned at the stake as a witch, because she was thought to have special powers, sadly, mainly working with wild healing herbs.

This made Miriam think of Tallulah. And no, she had not found any reference to an ancient river or corn growing in the area.

Joanne had her own small car and arranged to meet up with various old school friends, mainly on Barton beach, while she was back home, but promised Miriam she would be there when her grandparents, Bill and Irene, returned from their travels the following Friday, although they just might want to spend some time in their New Milton house first, recovering.

Jeremy decided it would be a lot less 'stuffy' if the family all met up for evening dinner at 'Riches,' and booked a table for 7.30pm on the following Saturday. Both Lady Jane and Miriam were more than happy to have someone else preparing the food, as there was a lot to discuss with Miriam's parents.

Bill and Irene Robinson returned home exhausted on the Friday, as expected. They were very pleased to hear that a table had been booked for Saturday evening in Bournemouth, as they wanted to talk to Lady Jane to see how the arrangements were progressing and to thank her for all her hard work. Miriam had been able to explain quite a lot over the phone and they had transferred money over for wedding flowers and the brides and bridesmaids' dresses, but Irene especially wanted to make sure she paid her share of costs.

They met up with their daughter and grand-daughter on the Saturday morning and complimented Miriam straight away, saying how well she looked and how much they had missed both their 'girls,' although visiting foreign parts had been pretty wonderful.

Saturday evening dinner at 'Riches' was a great success, with all six soon-to-be relatives sat around the table; - Jeremy, Lady Jane, Miriam, Joanne, Bill and Irene. Richard Perriment, who was delighted to be asked to be Jeremy's best man, joined them briefly for coffee, and received many compliments on the good food his chef had produced.

There would be a wedding rehearsal at the church on the next Wednesday evening. Jeremy made the decision to close the Unicorn over the whole bank holiday, until the following Wednesday, to give all his staff a break to enjoy the wedding together.

No staff were invited to Jeremy's first wedding to Caroline in Romsey Abbey, just relatives and her titled associates from the London area, so Jeremy wanted this wedding to be very different, with the church ceremony and evening party opened up to all, including any villagers who wanted to come.

The wedding breakfast was under Lady Jane's strict control; invited guests only. Miriam was slightly worried there might be an element of trouble in the evening, but this did not deter Jeremy, saying there was nothing that himself and Richard could not sort out between them!

The live music and hog roast for the evening party would finish at 10pm sharp, ending with a firework display, arranged by Alan, who 'knew someone in the trade.'

Miriam had a surprise phone call from Lady Jane during the week. Cerys had been in touch to see if her twin, four-year-old grand-daughters could possibly be flower-girls at the wedding. Little Rose and Poppy would wear cream satin frocks with pink sashes, if Miriam approved. Her answer was,

'Why not? I'm sure Joanne will be happy to supervise two more.'

Miriam planned to make up her own bouquet and the bridesmaids' posies, herself and could easily find two small baskets for her flower girls to carry. Susan and the other church flower arrangers had offered to decorate the church, including an arch of roses over the main entrance.

The 28th August dawned sunny and warm. At 10am precisely, Alice joined Joanne and Miriam, with Jenny, who was going to be their hair and make-up artist, in Miriam's cottage. Sandwiches, fruit, white wine and orange juice were passed round as mid-day approached. Alice's normally straight fair hair was coaxed into gentle waves to match in with Joanne's.

The bride decided not to pin her hair up and by the time Jenny had finished, all three looked beautiful, with Miriam especially radiant, her hair and skin glowing with health and only the lightest touch of make-up.

The cream, lace over satin, midi-length wedding dress fitted perfectly, strapless with a lacy cream bolero to cover her shoulders in church. Rose and Poppy called in to collect their flowers.

All of them wore pink and mauve rosebuds in clips and bands in their hair. Miriam had to relent a little on her colour theme as she was the only one to find cream coloured shoes. The bridesmaids all wore white sandals.

As Rose and Poppy headed out with their parents, Miriam donned her 'something borrowed,' a set of cultured pearls including pearl earrings from Lady Jane. Jenny gave her a saucy blue garter and Irene had found her a very old silver bracelet, which had belonged to her grandmother.

Alan came to collect Jenny just after 2pm, followed by the bridesmaids' car at 2.15pm, taking Irene with them. At 2.25pm Bill's heart swelled with pride, as he looked at his beautiful daughter, about to marry 'the lord of the manor,' which was how he saw Jeremy.

'No regrets, Lass?' he asked.

'Definitely no regrets, Dad!' she replied, as they got into the wedding car.

'At one time, I felt I was being disloyal to David's memory, but now I know he would want me to have this joy back in my life. We made some happy memories in the past and I believe I can make more with Jeremy, in the future, from today onwards.'

Bill grinned at her, as their car pulled away from the cottage.

The village church was packed. Jeremy and Richard, nervously awaiting the bride's arrival, checked the wedding rings for the ninth time. They wore matching outfits of dark grey suits, cream shirts and pink ties with buttonholes of pink rosebuds.

Reverend Patricia Armstrong walked forward, inviting the bridegroom and his best man to stand and walk into the aisle, as the organist struck up the bridal march.

There were gasps of admiration from the congregation, as Bill led his beautiful daughter up the aisle, followed by Joanne and Alice in their pink gowns and Rose and Poppy in their little cream satin frocks with pink sashes, all wearing Celtic gold cross necklaces, a present from the groom and carrying rosebud posies, prepared by the bride.

Jeremy was stunned, just gazing at his beautiful bride. The couple had chosen two cheerful hymns, 'Morning Has Broken' and 'Love Divine, All Loves Excelling.' As the service progressed, vows and rings were exchanged and the love Miriam and Jeremy felt for each other shone out, reaching all around them. The vicar felt there was a true sense of God being there with them, in her church.

Miriam knew she had already been blessed with the most wonderful miracle, which she had yet to share with Jeremy. There was a reason why her whole body glowed with health.

Afterwards, they posed for photographs beneath the arch of roses. Joy had brought six of her pre-school four year olds to throw rose petal confetti over the bride and groom. Tallulah's daughter, Zoe, from the stables, had laid on a horse-drawn carriage to take the newlyweds to their reception, ahead of the wedding cars.

Jeremy and Miriam got their first proper look at the rest of the congregation. Only the mother of the groom, Lady Jane, was wearing a hat, mauve silk to match her outfit, although the bride's mother, Irene, had a dark pink 'fascinator' in her hair, complimenting her dark pink dress and jacket.

Outstandingly smart were Piers and Lucas. Not

so much Lucas, as his cream suit and mulberry shirt seemed quiet, compared to Piers' jacket and trousers in bright mulberry, with a cream shirt, but so immaculate and upmarket that everyone was seriously impressed with his choice of colour and style.

Miriam tossed her bouquet in the air and it was caught by Jenny!

'That's it!' Jenny said to Alan, 'Our turn next!'

Zoe steadied the white horse, as the couple climbed into their open carriage, to drive on to their reception at the manor. Miriam remarked that she did not realize just how many people there were, living in Cornhaven.

Many shouted, 'Congratulations!' and 'See you in the barn this evening!' as they passed by.

The caterers had done a sterling job. The marquee looked beautiful, festooned with cream and pink ribbon and flowers. Sixty guests were catered for, with a varied choice of food from hot roast pheasant with roast vegetables to cold, sliced breaded gammon and a selection of salads. There was freshly baked bread and vegetable soup or pate on offer for those wanting a starter. Everyone was free to order what they wanted from the smiling waiters, collecting the food from a side buffet. Unusual for a wedding breakfast, but it worked well, as everyone found something they enjoyed.

Dessert was a modern take on fresh fruit salad and meringue with cream, or ice-cream for the children, if they wanted.

Jeremy recognized Richard's style in the catering and told him he had done a brilliant job, although the caterers were not employed by him.

Sitting at the head table were Lady Jane, Irene, Bill, Joanne, Alice and Richard with the bride and groom. Little flower girls, Rose and Poppy sat immediately in front of them, with their parents and grand-parents. Miriam was pleased to see that Jed had at least agreed to come to the reception, sat at a table with Clive, Betty, Joe and their daughters.

'What is wrong with Jed?' Miriam asked Lady Jane.

'It's a long, sad story,' she replied. 'He never got over losing his one true love, over seventy years ago. He was living in London back then, a trainee accountant, very much in love with a shop girl, Bethany. She lived with her mother on the east side and the story goes that there was an explosion, destroying her home overnight.

Jed was devastated. That's when he took the decision that, after finishing his exams, he would move down here. My father-in-law, Sir Arthur, needed an accountant and took Jed on. He's been here ever since. Good at his job, but very secretive.'

'That's ever so sad,' Miriam replied. 'Looks like there's no joy in his life without Bethany.'

The bride's father and the best man gave their speeches. Richard recalled a few cheeky incidences from when he was at Oxford university with Jeremy, which went down well with the guests and the bride!

Jeremy thanked everyone profusely and the happy couple received many a toast to their future together.

Alice was delighted to learn that her bridesmaid's outfit was hers to keep for good.

Lauren, Mark and their son, Oliver, sitting with Malcolm, Jill, Alan, Jenny, Tom and Susan, all agreed it was the best wedding they had ever been to, except perhaps their own!

At 6pm precisely, the music started up in the barn and Jeremy and Miriam led their guests across for their first dance as a married couple. The hog roast was underway, and by 6.30pm people were trickling in from Cornwood, to join the party.

Some of the afternoon guests gave their thank-yous and left, including Rose and Poppy's parents, who had to head back to the farm in Wales with their girls, who were due to start their new school later that week. They were thanked profusely for their contribution to the day.

Cerys and Bryn were staying on, with rooms booked at the Royal Bath Hotel in Bournemouth, for several nights. Jeremy learned that they had booked a room for his mother to join them, too, allowing the newlyweds to have the whole house to themselves, before leaving on honeymoon, the following morning.

Jeremy had something on his mind. He had an important secret of his own he must now share with his wife. Miriam wanted to talk to him privately too, as they had both been surrounded by other people all day.

Almost unconsciously, they held hands and quietly left the barn. Checking that no-one was following, Jeremy led Miriam towards the back gate, leading to the forest path.

'There's someone I must introduce to you, my help and advisor for many years,' Jeremy began.

'Jeremy, just let's stop for a minute,' Miriam answered, as they reached the oak tree, where they had first become physically united.

'You remember our first night together?' she began, smiling excitedly, 'well, I felt at the time that there is a tremendous, magical sense of healing in this forest and it's been proved true.

I found out for sure this morning that we have been blessed with a very special miracle.' She took his right hand and placed it close to her waistline.

'You don't mean - - - - - a baby!!!!' Jeremy jumped in the air as she nodded.

'My Darling, what a wonderful wedding present! All my dreams have come true, today! Thank-you, my angel. I must take good care of you especially from now on.'

'Jeremy, I've never felt healthier and stronger,' Miriam replied. 'It's so different from when I had Joanne. I was so poorly back then.'

They walked on, arms round each other, until they arrived at a metal gate in the path. Jeremy opened the gate, using an electronic key.

Noric

The gate automatically closed behind them. Walking on, about ten paces, Jeremy stopped on the path and asked Miriam to look to her left and tell him what she could see.

'Just more conifer trees,' Miriam began, 'but hang on a minute, it looks as though there's another pathway through here and it's lighter beyond these trees.'

Jeremy smiled, seeming somehow relieved of his anxiety, as she led the way down the narrow pathway.

'Oh Wow! What a pretty picture!' Miriam exclaimed, as the pathway stopped at the top of a gentle slope, leading down to an open area of grassland, surrounded by trees.

There appeared to be another village, small cottages and a stream, at the far side of the grassland, where animals were grazing. She saw deer, foxes, squirrels and white ponies, like something out of a child's picture book, just there, together.

Suddenly, one of the white ponies turned to face Jeremy and Miriam and started walking towards them, only 'pony' was the wrong name for this beautiful, majestic creature, a full-sized horse with a golden horn - a unicorn!

'Your father's drawing from his Sunday school days!' Miriam exclaimed to Jeremy.

'He's so beautiful.'

'Don't be surprised at his next move,' Jeremy smiled, as the unicorn approached them, 'this is Noric.'

The sturdy yet graceful animal bowed his head to the couple, then to Miriam's amazement he spoke!

'Congratulations to both of you,' he began in

a deep, gentle voice, 'Miriam, welcome to my land, to ancient Cornhaven, the haven of the unicorns. Thank-you for visiting us. This part of the land is and always has been, ours. Jeremy is now our guardian, keeping this land free for our use and I am his counselor and adviser, when he needs guidance. The whole forest is a place with healing powers. But I think you know this. A little bird tells me you have had great news.'

'WHAT 'little bird?' Jeremy asked, fearing the worst, could it be Jed yet again.

Noric looked him in the eye, 'Gordon, the green woodpecker. He lives in the old oak tree and probably heard you talking.'

'Oh, that's all right then,' Jeremy replied, as his wife collapsed in a fit of giggles.

'Are you the reason we see those white lights over the forest, mainly in the summer months?' Miriam asked. 'Alan says it's U.F.Os.'

'Meaning, Unicorns Flying Over?' Noric asked.

'No, unicorns can't fly. The white lights are a form of earth energy being drawn upwards to the sky. Totally harmless. By the way, when it comes to choosing names for your little one, our future guardian, how about Nor, Urni, Ron or Nic?'

'I see; anything made from the letters of the word unicorn?' grinned Miriam. 'We might just have a few ideas of our own. But thanks, all the same. Is what I'm seeing real?'

'You are looking into my world, Miriam,' Noric's gentle voice continued. 'We offer peace, healing and a place of escape from your troubled world. But it is important that not everyone knows about my world, as there are those who would destroy it. This is why, over many hundreds of years, we have chosen sympathetic human beings to protect us. Promise me you will keep this between yourself and Jeremy.'

'Of course I will,' Miriam replied. 'This is pure magic to me. I expected to end up walking onto farmland worked by Jeremy's tenants, to the right of the forest, or end up in the riding stables, to the left.

'What a wonderful, hidden valley you have here.'

As a mist started to rise from the far side of ancient Cornhaven, Jeremy took Miriam's hand and said, 'Thank-you Noric, but we must leave now and return to our guests.'

'In a year's time,' the unicorn said, 'return with your little one. I want to meet our future guardian.'

'I promise we will bring the baby to see you,' Jeremy replied.

As they walked back down the woodland path and through the gate, Miriam noticed how quiet her husband had become.

'That was truly amazing,' she said to him, 'but you seem distracted. Is anything wrong?'

'Far from it,' he replied. 'You know, six years ago I brought Caroline here to meet Noric and she saw nothing but trees. I'm so very lucky to have you, to know you have the gift too and will not make fun of me.'

'Oh Jeremy,' she replied, 'I love you so very much. I'm proud to be your wife and even more proud to be expecting your baby - - - - - except - -

'Except what?' Jeremy looked worried.

'Well, it won't arrive with four hooves and a tail, will it?' she had a mischievous grin on her face.

'No, Darling, I'm quite sure this one will be 100% human,' he replied. ' Might have a horn, though!'

'You're wicked!' Miriam shouted, hugging him tightly, enjoying the feel of his firm body against hers.

'By the way, where exactly are we going tomorrow for our honeymoon? Joanne helped me pack my bags yesterday and said I might need my passport.'

'Right then. How about a little quiz. We will be heading off to somewhere involving a longish drive, short flight, blue seas, white sands, tropical plants and beginning with the letter 'T'.' Jeremy said, smiling at the thought.

Miriam frowned,

'Can't be the Isle of Wight then, or the Channel Isles. Oh Jeremy, it's not Tresco, Is it? I've always wanted to go back to the Scilly Isles. Haven't been back since I was thirteen, when I went with Mum and Dad on the Scillonian ferry!'

'Your wish is my command, my love. That's exactly where we ARE going. Ten nights in our own cottage with full use of the facilities at the Island Hotel, then one night in St. Ives, before we return home.' Jeremy was very happy to see how delighted she was.

Returning through the gate at the back of the manor house, Jeremy could hear singing coming from the conservatory, where his mother had decided to position herself, 'guarding' the wedding presents, which were there on display.

As they rounded the corner, Jeremy and Miriam saw her, hat askew over one eye and swigging the remains of a bottle of champagne, as she waved it in the air, singing raucously, to the tune of 'here we go round the mulberry bush.'

'My Jeremy's been a naughty boy,
A naughty boy, a naughty boy,
My Jeremy's been a naughty boy,
And I will be a Grand – Ma!'

Miriam and Jeremy looked at each other, then burst out laughing.

'There's no way she could know yet,' Miriam said, 'you're the first one I've told!'

'Don't worry,' Jeremy replied, 'but I can see your daughter's beckoning to you by the old stables, so you sort yours out while I deal with mine.'

As Jeremy approached the conservatory, a somewhat agitated Cerys approached him.

'Everything's fine, Jeremy,' she said. 'Bryn's just taken your mother's case to our car and we'll head off to the Royal Bath hotel in Bournemouth, just as soon as we can get her loaded.'

'Looks like she's already 'loaded,' Jeremy replied, 'I've never seen her like that before.'

'I think she got hold of some gin, earlier,' Cerys said. 'Now come on Janice, we're ready to go on to Bournemouth. Tomorrow we've booked tickets to see 'Blithe Spirit,' I know how much you enjoy Noel Coward. Oh, Jeremy, just to let you know that Tom and Susan have taken Hector to their house, so he won't be frightened by the fireworks later. Tom says they'll pop round to see you off at 9am tomorrow, so you and Miriam will have the whole house to yourselves tonight. We'll return your mother on Friday.'

'Thank-you, Aunty Cerys. This is so good of you,' Jeremy replied, as he helped his mother into Bryn's car.

Meanwhile, Miriam met up with Joanne, who had a furtive expression on her face.

'Oh Mum,' Joanne began, 'I thought you might need your anorak to watch the fireworks later, so I've fetched it from the cottage. The thing is, Gran was there clearing up from earlier and she found something in the rubbish. Mum, she's accusing me of being pregnant! Said you were unable to have another baby, so it couldn't be you taking that test.'

'Joanne, I'm so sorry. I wanted Jeremy to be the first to know and yes, we have our own little miracle on the way, sometime next spring. I'd better have a word with your gran now. Jeremy's absolutely over the moon. We both are,' Miriam said, smiling, 'but we were hoping to keep it quiet for a bit longer yet.'

'As long as you're happy, Mum, then I am too. Goodness, I'll be nineteen then. Wow, a big sister at last at nineteen!' Joanne looked joyful at the thought.

'Oh, it is OK if I have a couple of friends stay over at the cottage with me, isn't it? Promise I'll clean up afterwards.'

'Of course, darling. I trust you,' Miriam agreed. After all, the cottage would soon belong to Joanne anyway.

Richard, his wife, Celeste and their two children, Molly and Marcus were in the barn with Lauren, Mark and Oliver, when Miriam and Jeremy returned to see their guests, watching the band playing favourite rock dance music.

The children joined in the dancing with others from the village.

Richard signaled to Jeremy that he wanted to speak to him outside, away from the noise.

'Glad you're both back from your walk,' Richard

began. 'Alan's suggested bringing the firework display forward to 9.30pm, as some of the evening guests have left.'

'That's fine by me,' Jeremy replied, smiling. 'It has been such a wonderful day for us. By the way, I was wondering how you and Celeste would feel about being asked to be godparents next spring?'

'What! You crafty old fox!' Richard exclaimed.

'An heir to the Wilberforce-Smythe estate on the way all ready? Congratulations! When did you find out?'

'Miriam's only just had a positive test and we didn't intend telling anyone for at least another month, but we're both so very happy. It's a real miracle, as she was told there would be no more babies after Joanne was born,' Jeremy replied, his eyes misting over.

Richard looked quizzical. 'I wonder,' he began, 'if that old man who works for you, Jed, is it? knew somehow. I saw him coming in through the back gate and talking to your mother, just before she started singing about being a granny.'

'That would not surprise me in the least,' Jeremy replied, 'he's getting to be a bit of a nuisance, upsetting various people. Something to sort out after our honeymoon, I think. Trouble is, how? He's been with the family so many years, since my grand-father took pity on him. Sees himself as my mother's informant.

He's 92, you know. Thought he'd be long gone by now.'

'Well, if there's ever anything I can do, just let me know,' Richard said, 'but for now, here's hoping you two have a wonderful time in the Scilly Isles. Oh, by the way, the caterers have cleared the marquee and Alan, Malcolm and Tom have all said they'll be round to do any final clearing up needed, later tomorrow. Lauren and Joanne will be checking up on the garden centre plants, ready to re-open on Wednesday. They're a good team of people, Jeremy, to your credit, I think.'

At 9.30pm precisely, the band stopped playing and everyone headed outside to watch the fireworks.

Jeremy and Miriam stood alone watching the display from the front steps of the manor house. As the final rocket exploded in the sky, they waved goodbye to their guests. Jeremy carried his bride over the threshold, locking the front door behind them. Their married life had begun.

Into September

Wednesday morning at the Unicorn found Betty, Malcolm, Alan and Lauren holding an impromptu meeting of their own, before opening the garden centre to customers.

'Well,' Betty began, 'that's that then, but wasn't it a lovely wedding? Never seen Miriam looking so beautiful. The food was good, too.'

'Joanne was at the house with Tom yesterday, to see them off on honeymoon,' Lauren added . 'Looks like she's spoilt for choice where to live from now on, what with Jeremy offering her a room at the manor and her mother saying she can have the cottage.'

'Our Alice was thrilled to be asked to be a bridesmaid,' Malcolm joined in, 'Miriam's so kind – hearted.'

'The caterers and marquee people were very efficient,' Alan added. 'It's all cleared away, now, there wasn't much for us to do at all, yesterday. Tom's keeping Hector at their place until Friday, when Lady Jane returns.'

'She went a bit funny, didn't she?' Betty remarked, 'singing away in the conservatory, ranting on about being a grandma. Sad though, because Miriam was told she can't have any more babies.'

Lauren was grinning,

'I'm not so sure about that, Betty. Joanne let something slip yesterday about being needed at the manor after next spring. We'll just have to wait and see.'

At 9am, Alan unlocked the gates and soon afterwards the first customers started drifting in from the car park. Lauren was glad she had had Joanne's help for a couple of hours the previous day, when the garden centre was closed, to keep the plants in tip-top condition. Piers and Lucas were away on holiday until the following Wednesday, mainly sailing.

Lauren, Mark and Oliver had managed a week away, staying on the Isle of Wight, earlier in August, showing Oliver Osborne House, Blackgang Chine and the Needles, in good, warm weather.

That particular morning, Mark had taken Oliver with him, to measure up a client's garden for a new landscaping scheme, while Lauren was at work.

Clive was staying on for a couple of weeks more, before starting his horticultural degree course at Bath university, which he was really looking forward to, with Lauren's encouragement. Joanne had decided to spend some time helping Zoe up at the riding stables, but said she would be willing to work at the garden centre, if needed. Joanne enjoyed talking to Zoe about the things her mother, Tallulah used to get up to with Joanne's grandmother, Irene, thirty odd years previously. Zoe was just a few years younger than Miriam.

Lauren was called on by Betty to help a customer, later that morning. Mrs. Radstock, a nervous, middle aged lady, needed advice on buying clematis.

'It's for my father's garden,' she said. 'I want a plant that produces double flowers in blue or purple, to grow close to a white climbing rose.'
Lauren suggested the variety, 'Vyvyan Pennel' might fit the bill, after spending some time discussing the various options with Mrs. Radstock.

Unfortunately larger plants of that variety were

sold out, but Lauren managed to find a younger one in a freshly delivered batch, with flower buds, as it often flowered twice a year. The customer seemed happy with her choice and took on board Lauren's advice on the right position and soil for the climber.

Visitor numbers were dropping off, now the bank holiday was over, although the coffee shop remained very busy. Julie and Shirley had taken over caring for Pussy Willow, now fully established as the Unicorn's 'guard cat,' proving his worth in keeping mice at bay. Willow was allowed in the outside seating area of the coffee shop but not where food was prepared and served indoors. The visiting children loved him.

Betty's husband, Joe, had been given good news about his job with the railway company. It looked like he was safe for at least another year, but they wanted him to consider re-training to take on an administrative roll. Betty was relieved that he had agreed to do this.

With Clare away as well as Piers and Lucas, the staff were a bit thin on the ground. Lauren asked Clive to mainly look after the water garden section, while she was busy with both houseplants and the outside plant area.

Around midday, Malcolm alerted Lauren to the fact that the 'Grey's Green Gardens' van had turned up in the main car park. Her blood ran cold, dreading the thought that maybe one of the women who had tried to steal the pond pumps, was back.

However, this time there was no sign of her, only a man in the van, who appeared to be eating his lunch. Shortly after,

Lauren was surprised to see Mark and Oliver crossing the yard. Mark suggested perhaps the three of them could have lunch together in the coffee shop, as there was something he wanted to tell her. After checking that Malcolm was in the yard and Clive was happy to man the water garden section, Lauren headed off for lunch with her family.

When the three of them had sat down around one of the outside tables, in the sun, Mark expressed his concerns.

'The thing is,' he began, 'you know we went to measure up that plot this morning for Mrs. Baker, over near Mottisfont? Well, it turns out she's already had one quote from a company based down here, in New Milton. She let slip what it was for and honestly, it is way below what I would have to charge just for materials.

I'm wondering if you know them. Call themselves 'Grey's Green Gardens' or '3 Gs?' Mrs. Baker wants a fair bit of hard landscaping work carried out, including building a rockery and paved patio and I don't know how they can charge so little and still make a living.'

'That's worrying,' replied Lauren, as Julie brought their lunch to the table. 'Malcolm's been watching a 'Grey's Green Gardens' van in the car park, this morning. It was only a few weeks ago that two women tried to steal pond pumps from here and one of them got into that van. I only hope Jeremy's security system holds while he's away with Miriam. I believe if anyone does try to break into the yard, the police will be alerted, after hours. Glad you and Oliver dropped in, as we need to be very watchful from now on.

After lunch and after Oliver had finished making a fuss of Willow, Mark took his son into New Milton to buy some new shoes, ready for school starting the following week. Lauren passed her latest news onto Malcolm and Betty, who agreed that all staff needed to be extra vigilant. Alan said he would walk round the garden centre after closing, at random times with Jenny, to see if anything unusual happened.

'What about Jed?' Malcolm asked Lauren.

'Should he be informed?'

'I'm not sure that's necessary, because he's so old. What could he do anyway?' Lauren replied.

'Also, so far there's so little to go on. Let's just hang on for a bit, but keep watch.'

The remainder of the week passed by without incident. On Sunday, Tom and Alan volunteered to check up on the garden centre and check with Lady Jane that all was well up at the manor, although she had help from her housekeeper Ruth, when needed.

Lady Jane had her own, self-contained wing in the house, but the conservatory was shared by both sections. Hector spent most of his elderly doggy life on his bed in the conservatory, or Lady Jane's kitchen, in colder weather. Tom often took him out for his daily walks, although sometimes Lady Jane would walk Hector herself.

Jed, having been given strict instructions from Jeremy that under no circumstances was he to bother the staff with extra paper work, resigned himself to maintaining paper records in his office and visiting the coffee shop daily for his tea and cake.

He too had noticed the '3Gs' van back in the car park and felt it was his duty to inform Lady Jane, now she had returned from Bournemouth, but only received an abrupt reply that the other staff would deal with any potential problem and 'no,' under no circumstances was Jeremy to be bothered while away on honeymoon.

The weekend passed by quietly, but on the following Monday morning Lauren was accosted by a very upset Mrs. Radstock, returning the clematis she had bought.

'This is useless, absolutely useless!' she began.

'Look, the bud has opened and the flower is single, NOT double, as I had asked!'

Lauren was puzzled for a moment, then realized what had happened.

'I'm very sorry if it's not right for you,' she said,

'but this variety does produce its main flowers, which are definitely double, in early summer. What you get now is a second flowering and some of these flowers will be single.'

'Well, what good is that!' Mrs. Radstock was very agitated, 'My father is over 90 and might not live to see it flower next summer!'

Lauren felt exasperated. All she could do was offer a refund or replace the clematis with another plant, but there could be no guarantee that any clematis would produce double flowers before the following spring or early summer.

'What I could try and do for you, is to phone our suppliers, to see if they have any specimen sized plants left, with double flowers, but honestly this is the wrong time of year for them,' Lauren explained.

Mrs. Radstock agreed to this, but also accepted a refund, which Lauren arranged with Betty.

Later in the day, Lauren received a phone call back from Nightingale nurseries, not very far from her home in the Romsey area, to say they had found a specimen sized Vyvyan Pennel, returned from a commercial display, showing some single and some double flowers. Would it be suitable? If so, Lauren could have it for her customer if she was able to collect it from them.

It would be over three times the price of the young plant previously sold to Mrs. Radstock, but Lauren decided to accept it anyway. Alan offered to collect the plant in its 20 litre pot the next day, as it was far too big for Lauren's car boot and needed a van to move it

When it arrived back at the garden centre on the Tuesday morning, Lauren was delighted. It was a beautiful, healthy climber on a wooden frame in its pot. Her customer called in later in the day, and was much happier with the plant, which Alan then delivered to its new garden for her.

Meanwhile, on a distant island, far, far away, a certain pair of lovers were enjoying a most wonderful honeymoon. The weather was holding warm and sunny for them. Miriam had enjoyed the fifteen minute helicopter flight from Penzance, over the deep blue sea, direct to Tresco, looking down on green fields and white, sandy beaches, as they came into land.

They were escorted to a comfortable, neat holiday cottage, where Jeremy had arranged a basic grocery delivery to be waiting for them and later enjoyed dinner at the Island hotel, recently totally renovated.

Their days were spent exploring Tresco and visiting the other islands in the group, including St. Marys, St. Martins, St Agnes and Bryher. From St Marys, they could watch gig boat racing across the bay, or go out wildlife spotting, if they felt adventurous, watching puffins and seals.

But mostly they enjoyed the sheer beauty of Tresco, especially the Abbey gardens, with its sub-tropical plants and scampering red squirrels. Miriam remembered the large statue of the Earth goddess, Gaia, in the gardens.

'I might look like her, in a few months' time!' she quipped.

'I think she's very beautiful,' Jeremy replied.

There were still sky larks dive – bombing anyone who might venture near their nests beside the old fort, which Miriam also remembered from her visit as a teenager.

If they felt hot, they would paddle in the azure sea, watching fishing boats and ferry boats coming into shore. The flower farm on St. Martins island interested Miriam, as they made a living from selling early narcissi, boxed, by post to the mainland during winter and spring and pinks or carnations in the summer months.

The other flowers that fascinated her were the islands' amaryllis belladonna lilies, sometimes sold as nerines, lovely, tall pinkish lily flowers in late summer. She found some bulbs for sale from a roadside stall and bought three to take back home.

After dinner, they would watch the setting sun before gratefully spending blissful, idyllic nights in each other's arms, listening to the sea splashing on the rocks in the bay, beyond their cottage.

'Promise me we will come back again,' Miriam murmured to her husband.

'Just try and stop me!' he grinned. 'These have been the most wonderful days of my whole life. Of course we'll be back, baby too!'

Trouble

It happened the night before Jeremy and Miriam were due back at The Unicorn.
Sergeant Sandy MacAlister was on duty, when the alarm sounded at 1am.

A phone call came through from Covert Cameras main depot, to confirm that the alarm was activated at the Unicorn garden centre, about three miles from the police station.

The Scotsman rounded up his team of three stalwart officers to head out to meet the security company guys at the garden centre, having first phoned Alan, who was taking any emergency calls while Jeremy was away and lived just about a mile from the garden centre.

Earlier, during the afternoon, Malcolm had noticed an unmarked flatbed truck parked in the lay-by, outside the garden centre, where a previous repair in the boundary fencing had been carried out by himself and Alan.

There appeared to be no-one with the truck at the time, so Malcolm thought no more of it, as it was a free public space, after all.

Alan called Malcolm and the two of them arrived together at the scene, just ahead of the police and security firm men. What they saw, stunned them totally.

Yes, there was an opening in in the boundary between the truck and the garden centre yard, close to displays of rockery stone and chippings. BUT - - - - what on Earth?!!!

Overhead there were concentric circles of silent, neon blue and white, pulsating lights. For a few seconds, a rhythmic 'whooo' sound hit them, then stopped altogether. The lights appeared to be hovering over a security camera, fitted by Covert Camera's men, just a few months previously.

Standing totally unable to move, beside a pallet of rockery stone, which had been broken open, were two men dressed in black hooded jackets and jeans, just staring into space. Sergeant MacAlister sent his men forward to apprehend the two suspects and take them back to the police cells, in handcuffs.

'Looks like our new system works well,' Giles from the security company remarked to Alan, who had been convinced he was watching an unidentified flying object overhead.

'Looks like those men were totally mesmerized by the lights. Mind you, I thought our device only gave off a blue light to show where the break-in occurred. That white light's a bit weird,' Giles continued.

'Not sure that what you have here is exactly legal, bearing in mind the state of the suspects,' MacAlister commented. 'We will need to speak with Sir Jeremy, as soon as he returns.'

With that, he quickly taped off the scene of crime for his officers to examine more closely in daylight, leaving it up to Alan, Malcolm and Giles to block the opening in the boundary fence.

By now, Giles had stopped and reset the alarm, checking first that the close circuit TV footage was marked and safe from being deleted.

'So, when is the boss back?' Giles asked Alan.

'Sometime tomorrow, or perhaps I should say later today,' Alan replied.

'He's been away on honeymoon for almost two weeks.'

'Right, I'll talk to him early next week,' Giles replied. 'In the meantime once we've blocked up this gap, I'll reactivate the alarm when we leave the yard.'

Alan and Malcolm decided against disturbing Lady Jane, as it was now nearly 3am Saturday morning. They had wired in some temporary fencing to close off the broken old gateway, locked the yard entrance and headed back to their homes, after Giles too had left the scene.

Lucas was horrified when he came into work later that morning, to see evidence of the break-in. Only the day before, he had taken delivery of rockery stone and paving slabs, intended for the various projects he was working on, including the Chelsea flower show garden for the following May. Luckily, nothing had been taken.

Lauren and Clive arranged large flower pots to deter customers from trying to go past the police tape, until the scenes of crime officers had finished their work. The two men held in custody after their arrest claimed to have no memory of the incident, denying any wrong-doing, although it was obvious they had been caught red-handed, having forced their way into the yard.

Lady Jane herself came down to speak with the police officers later that morning, saying she would phone Jeremy and Miriam, who had spent the previous night in St. Ives.

She told Jeremy not to feel they needed to rush back, as everything was under control, thanks largely to the systems Jeremy had put in place for such an emergency.

After Tom told her what had happened, Joanne came over to offer her help. She had previously suggested to Lady Jane that she would prepare a meal for the four of them that evening, when her mother and step-father would be back at the manor. Lady Jane was happy to agree, so Joanne had made one of her special beef hot-pots for them all, as taught by Miriam.

Jeremy and Miriam arrived back at The Unicorn during late afternoon, to survey the damage. The police had fortunately finished their work in the yard and along the garden centre boundary walling and fencing. Jeremy got onto sergeant MacAlister straight away, to get the whole story and was informed that the men arrested, still denying any offence, were linked to 'Greys Green Gardens' landscapers, as sub-contractors.

'Hopefully we've got enough evidence to convict them, especially since seeing your close circuit TV footage of the event,' the policeman told Jeremy, who was now very concerned about getting proper rebuilding work carried out on that side of the yard.

There was a problem concerning the dry stone walling, over on that side, which may or may not have a preservation order on it, demanding full, accurate, reconstruction.

Jeremy had hoped to replace all of it with metal security fencing. He could see a battle looming with either the parish, or district council planners.

Later that evening, Joanne served up her home-made dinner, complete with potato slices and freshly baked bread from Cornhaven bakery, to Lady Jane, Jeremy and Miriam, at the main dining table in the manor house.

Joanne had also prepared a trifle the day before, which she knew her mother loved. The dinner was warmly welcomed by everyone.

Afterwards, Lady Jane expressed her

apologies to the rest of the party, for her crazy behavior previously. It certainly was Jed, who had set her off, although she had to admit she had drunk far more than usual!

'You know,' Lady Jane began, 'I really do look forward to having a grand-child and welcome you, Joanne, as my step grand-daughter, but at the same time I realize Jed was well out of order, in his behavior.

I am worried about him. He's never been a happy individual, but seems to be becoming more and more obsessed with watching and following both you, Jeremy and Miriam. Do you think we could persuade him to see a doctor? I know, Jeremy, you have already tried to get him to modify his behavior.'

'I'll add it to my list, Mother,' Jeremy replied.

After they had finished their meal and cleared everything away, Joanne said she was heading back to the cottage.

'Church tomorrow,' Joanne said. 'I must be on time for the choir. Mum, will you be joining me, too?'

'I think we should all go to the morning service tomorrow,' Jeremy replied. 'We have a lot to be thankful for, after all.'

'Lovely. See you there at 10am,' Joanne smiled, as she left. 'Oh, I almost forget. Gran. And Granddad have booked a table for Sunday lunch for all of us, 1pm at the New Milton carvery, so no need to cook tomorrow!'

The following morning, after the church service, Lady Jane and Jeremy were able to meet up with Dorothy Marshall, head of the parish council, to get her thoughts on changing the garden centre boundary walls and fencing, but she could only advise Jeremy to discuss it with the district council. She was happy to let him have some contact details, however.

At 8.30am on the Monday morning, Jeremy and Miriam met up with the rest of the full-time employees in the garden centre shop, to discuss the break-in. Jeremy announced that he intended going ahead with getting full security fencing erected around the whole place, but would hopefully keep the dry stone walling on the outside. If necessary, he was prepared to fight his cause in court! He was more than happy with the system installed by Covert Cameras, but would look into whether or not to add further floodlighting.

During their honeymoon, the couple had discussed Miriam's new role at length. She still wanted to do some practical work and be involved in buying in the houseplants, but accepted that, more and more, she would be needed to take on Lady Jane's responsibilities in running her side of the estate, as well as the garden centre and would now have a desk in Lady Jane's office.

The couple decided they wanted to let everyone know there was a baby due the following spring, despite the fact that Miriam had yet to see her doctor and make arrangements for a scan. There were a lot of 'Wows' and 'Congratulations,' when the announcement was given by Jeremy, as well as grins and the odd giggle.

Autumn

Less than two weeks after the break-in, it was time for Joanne to head back to Manchester university, for year two of her degree course in anthropology and archaeology. She loaded her little car with everything needed for the new term, which also meant a change in accommodation to a shared student house. Luckily this had been arranged well in advance and she knew two of the three other students in the 'share.'

Jeremy, Miriam, Irene and Bill saw her off, making her promise to keep in touch regularly and saying they looked forward to having her back home for Christmas, or perhaps half-term, if she was free, then.

Miriam's doctor had booked her scan appointment at the local hospital for the following Monday, saying he thought she must be at least three months into her pregnancy, making her 'due' date close to Jeremy's fortieth birthday, at the end of March.

On the day of the scan, Jeremy went with her and they both marveled at their first glimpse on the scanner screen, of the little miracle they had started, making it's jerky movements. The technician gave the baby's development stage as twelve to thirteen weeks and presented them with a print-out picture to take away with them.

Back at the Unicorn, work was now well underway to install the new boundary security fencing, in sections, starting with the side that had sustained the break-in. Jeremy had found metalwork with a dark green plastic coating for the job, as he thought this would give him the security needed, without making it look like a prison yard. The mystery of the extra white, flashing lights remained, though Jeremy had some ideas of his own, as to who or what was responsible! Thank goodness his security measures had worked.

Lauren was busy in the yard, checking through a delivery of shrubs from top quality Liss Forest Nursery, when she saw Tom walking towards her.

'Hi Lauren. Mike and Barry Enfield have asked me if you and I would be interested in doing another 'Gardeners Questions' session, in a couple of weeks' time. I've sort of agreed. What do you think?'

'Well, yes,' Lauren replied, 'as long as Jeremy agrees too. Is there a theme for this one, or just general questions from the audience?'

'Could be anything, but I think it should be relevant for the time of year, don't you? Perhaps we could suggest questions on autumn planting or preparing for winter?' Tom wondered.

'Right. While you're here, just take a look at these shrubs. Aren't they fantastic? So strong and healthy, just crying out to be planted in warm, autumn soil, I think,' Lauren smiled.

When Jeremy returned, he called Lauren and Tom into his office, saying he had heard from the producers of the 'Gardeners Questions' programme and would be happy for them to do another show with the Enfield brothers in Cornhaven village hall.

This time, there would be a lady presenter, Lucy Bellingham, in charge. Lauren was a bit disappointed that Denzil Coombs would not be there and surprised to learn that he had now permanently retired.

However, there was good news waiting for Lauren, when she got home after work that day.

'Guess what?' Mark was jubilant. 'I got the Mottisfont job! Turns out 3Gs withdrew their offer and I've got the go ahead at my original quote!

'Pizza dinner tonight, everyone?'

Lauren, Mark and Oliver were delighted, as they tucked into their pizzas later. Lauren was hopeful that, with Greys Green Gardens out of the equation, Mark would win further contracts in the future, too. He might even need to take on staff, although he did have a tree surgeon friend who would help with any heavy work, if needed.

Late September into October tended to be a busy time for planning the following year's sales. Lauren had four or five nursery representatives coming to see her, in order to take bookings for special promotions of new varieties, plus a rough idea of the quantity of trees, shrubs and perennials needed.

Jeremy and Betty were looking into what had brought in the most money, regarding shop goods, including the pets department in conjunction with Piers and Lucas' look at the water gardening products.

Alan and Malcolm would put together their own report, in respect of other outdoor sales, including composts and pots, although it was Jeremy who dealt with the representatives from the various companies, to get the best deals. Miriam's houseplant department was left entirely up to her, but she did have discussions with Lauren, to decide just how many bedding plants and tender perennials they might need the following spring, with hanging-baskets in mind, which she still hoped she could work around the new baby's arrival.

Lauren thought it would be useful for herself

and Miriam to visit at least one
of their local bedding plant suppliers together, to
get a better idea of anything new on offer for
the following season, and this was arranged.

Tom and his wife, Susan, were long overdue
a holiday and booked a week away in
Guernsey, an easy flight from Southampton
airport. Tom made sure that both Ruth and Alan
were free to help Lady Jane at the manor, if
needed. Ruth had been housekeeper there since
Jeremy was ten years old and lived out, in a
cottage in Cornhaven, shared with her sister.
Neither of them had ever married.

Ruth mainly worked Monday to Friday and
Miriam was keen to see that she stayed on,
because she was easy to work with, in that big
house. Ruth also looked out for old Jed, who
lived alone in one of the remaining estate
cottages, on the edge of the village, often taking
him meals at the weekend.

Jeremy wanted to persuade Jed to see his
doctor, if only for a general check-up, but
thought that first of all he would set him, what
should be, a straightforward task, copying
highlighted sentences from a general report on
how the business had progressed that year.

It needed to be processed and typed, using a
simple computer word programme. Jed agreed,
but Jeremy sensed he was not at all happy. As
expected, it was a total disaster, with almost half
the highlighted parts missing in Jed's copy.
Jeremy booked a doctor's appointment for him,
the following week.

Two weeks flew by, and almost before she
knew it, Lauren was once again sitting up on
the village hall stage with Tom and the Enfield
brothers, ready for a second 'Gardeners

Questions.' The village hall was packed and Lucy Bellingham introduced herself to the panel and audience. Lauren would later describe her as a pleasant, thirty-something lady with long, dark hair and a good voice for radio.

The first question came from Callum, who admitted he had not owned a garden in the past and wanted some information on what he should be doing to get the most out of his new, tiny patch of ground. He was a keen sportsman and did not want to spend a lot of time gardening.

Lucy threw the question open to the panel, and Lauren offered to take it first.

'Congratulations, Callum on getting your first home with a garden,' she began. 'This is a very good time to get started, as the soil has warmed up through the summer months and is ideal for planting new container grown trees and shrubs, trees climbers and hardy perennials, as well as spring-flowering bulbs for next year.

However, different people want different things from their gardens, so perhaps you could start by making a list or rough drawing, of what you would like to see in your garden.'

Mike added, 'I would second that. Barry and I find that our clients want different things from their gardens at different stages in their lives and careers. For example, we've just carried out a major make-over on a garden that was mainly lawn for use by the couple's children and pets.

The owners now want a better, bigger patio and a lot more colour, in the way of flowering plants, since their children have grown up.'

Tom's opinion was that, if time was very limited, a straightforward patch of lawn with small shrubs and seasonal plants in pots might be an option, or at least a good start, until Callum felt more ambitious.

To add interest to a lawn for spring, part of the turf could be lifted and crocus, snowdrops or narcissus bulbs planted beneath it, to give a good show of colour.

Lucy thanked them for their answers and moved on to Diana, who needed some information on autumn colour and interest for her garden.

'My problem is that I'm not very successful when it comes to extending colour in my garden into autumn. I've tried growing Japanese Maples in pots, but they don't thrive.

Do you have any tips, please?' Diana asked the panel. Lucy suggested Lauren took this one.

'Well, Diana,' Lauren began, 'I feel there is more than one question here. First of all, there are other plants you can use, as well as Japanese Maples.

There are flowering plants such as Michaelmas daisies or asters, garden chrysanthemums and autumn flowering crocus or colchicums, which can add a splash of colour. Often dahlias, pansies or violas and nepeta or catmint will still be flowering now, too. When it comes to the beautiful, colourful leaves of acers, especially Japanese Maples, some years the weather is kinder to these than others. They do not like strong winds and will need some shelter, especially younger plants in pots.

Also, as I expect you already know, they need to be planted in ericaceous or lime-free compost and not be allowed to dry out at the root. If I could recommend only one Japanese Maple though, it would have to be the slow growing, umbrella shaped Acer palmatum Dissectum Atropurpureum,

with deep purple leaves throughout the growing

season. A mouthful of a name to say, but exceptional feathery leaf shape and colour. Looks lovely by a small garden pond, too.'

Wow!' Lucy commented, 'that's quite a lot to take in, Lauren. Perhaps we could move on to a question on planting trees, from Simon.'

'Good evening, panel,' Simon began, 'I would like some information on buying and planting both ornamental and fruit trees at this time of year. In the past, one would go along to a nursery earlier in the year, view young trees lined out in a field and select the right one for lifting and replanting in late autumn, as a bare-root tree. But this does not seem to be possible any more. Why?'

Tom had some answers to this one. 'Yes, we did used to grow trees like this, for anyone to reserve and buy a few years ago,' he began. 'In fact, there is a field next to the car park at the Unicorn garden centre which was used in this way only ten years ago. During the winter months, you may find root-wrapped small trees for sale in supermarkets, but most garden Centres now shy away from these because we feel our customers do better with pot grown plants, which have a better fibrous root system, to absorb water and nutrients from the soil. Also, field grown trees need a fair amount of care and maintenance, before they are ready to sell. There are still nurseries growing trees like this for commercial use, but not for sale to the general public. Many young trees may spend part of their early lives field grown by wholesalers, but are then potted up and grown on for garden centre sales, with many health checks along the way. When it comes to planting, first of all be happy with the plant you are buying. Make sure it is well-branched with a good root system. Dig a hole at least half as large again as the root ball and back fill around the roots with a mixture of soil, compost and bone meal, no deeper than the graft on the tree's stem or trunk.

Do not attempt to plant if the ground is frozen or water-logged and add a stake to support the tree, as it becomes established. Generally these days trees growing in pots can be planted in the ground at any time of year, but traditionally late autumn, when the soil is still warm but the tree is dormant, is best, giving your tree a head start on the next season.'

Barry raised his hand to question Simon as to whether there were any special varieties of trees he was looking for.

'Yes and no,' Simon replied. 'I have a large garden in need of more structure and my wife and I thought adding more height in the form of trees, would improve our outlook from the house. I suppose I am trying to find the most cost effective solution.'

Lucy thanked him and handed the microphone over to Angela, who was concerned about her allotment.

'I seem to have great difficulty growing onions, on my allotment. Everything else is fine. I'm self-sufficient in brassicas, potatoes and carrots and also get reasonable results with broad beans, runner beans, peas and lettuce, but onions fail terribly, mostly just going soft and rotting. What am I doing wrong?' Angela asked the panel.

Mike, a keen vegetable grower at home, offered to answer this one.

'Two thoughts in my mind, Angela,' he began, 'Onions are bulbs and prone to fungal attack, especially in overly wet ground, which can also spread the disease. Also, I had the same problem a few years ago and sorted it with constructing a raised bed, just for growing onions.

I used half-sized railway sleepers for the sides, which gave just enough height above the ground, when the centre was filled with a mix of new clean top-soil and bagged compost from the garden centre. Perhaps you could try this method yourself?'

'Thank-you, that's brilliant!' Angela replied. 'I'll certainly give it a go next season.'

There were further questions and answers on how to protect outdoor growing tree ferns and palm trees through winter, in coastal gardens and one very concerned member of the audience was battling with growing plants in dry, shady areas, partly under a conifer hedge.

Lauren had some suggestions for this one, backed up by Barry, who had recently planted up a similar area.

They suggested trying to improve the soil first, adding well-rotted farmyard manure or garden compost from a compost heap. Lauren said she had seen a vigorous, ground cover rose, Flower Carpet, used to good advantage planted three feet in front of a conifer hedge, then trained to grow towards the conIfers.

The list of plants suitable for growing in dry, shady areas included Gaultheria 'Shallon,' perennial Hypericum, Alchemilla mollis, Epimedium, Symphytum or Comfrey and Tellima grandiflora. Juniper Blue Star or Blue Carpet might also work, but would lose the blue colour, if too shaded.

Lauren added that whatever was planted, needed to be watered well in its first year, until the roots were well established.

Lucy thought they might just fit in one more question and Lionel raised his hand, to ask about fruit trees.

'I would like to know if the panel think it is possible to grow fruit trees in a very small garden?' he asked. There was an overwhelming

'Yes!' from the panel. Lauren said the criteria was the area of four paving slabs, preferably in sunlight. Another option might be to grow a fan-trained tree or an espalier, against a fence or wall. If there really was only room for a single tree, it was possible to buy either a 'family' apple or 'family' pear tree. Family apple trees generally consisted of three apple varieties, two eating, one cooking, grafted onto the same stem or trunk. October was a good month to buy these for choice of available varieties.

The evening ended on a high, with much applause for the panel. Lauren admitted that she felt a lot happier this time and less stressed, as it had gone so well. Lucy was able to inform them that the programme would go out on the air the following Tuesday evening. She thought virtually no editing would be needed and the sound was fine.

Mark, Susan, Miriam, Betty and Malcolm came over to congratulate the panel, especially Tom and Lauren, for their clear answers to the questions. Lauren realized that Jeremy was busy talking to Lucy and another young woman she did not recognize. They called her over.

'Lauren, I'd like you to meet Rachel Whitely, from our local commercial radio station.' Jeremy began. 'She would like you to take part in a fortnightly afternoon radio show with them, presenting a gardening topic and answering questions from listeners. I have already said the Unicorn garden centre would support this, in exchange for some free advertising, but it's up to you. Would you be interested?'

Yes, please!' Lauren replied. 'I've felt a lot more confident this evening and I think I could handle it now.'

'Good. That's settled then. Rachel will send us further details nearer the time. Thank-you, Lauren, I appreciate you taking this on,' Jeremy smiled, as they all left the hall, heading for The Fisherman's Rest.

Jed.

Jed just knew he had to protect the customers, especially any children. There was a lion loose in the garden centre! He had seen it himself, crouching down between the end of Lauren's shrub beds and the line of trees in pots, against Jeremy's new fence.

Perhaps he could drive it out of the yard, on his own, without bothering anyone else? Slowly, he crept along the path, towards the lion, fence post in hand.

Tallulah had parked her old van in the main car-park and was crossing the drive into the yard. Today, she was sensibly dressed in brown cord trousers, Aran sweater and an old anorak, because of the cooler, showery weather.

She was out to buy some feeding bowls, for her motley collection of animals at the sanctuary. She was the first to notice him and to wonder what on Earth he was up to!

Miriam was talking to Malcolm, who had been helping a customer load several bags of compost into their car, when they both saw Tallulah wave to them, pointing to one of the shrub beds, where they could see a fence post moving along, being carried by a certain elderly gentleman.

'What's he up to now!' Miriam exclaimed. 'He'll scare all our customers away.'

'I'll see if I can stop him,' Malcolm replied, walking slowly across the yard, trying to see what it was that Jed wanted to attack. Meanwhile, Miriam took out her phone to inform Jeremy of what was happening.

Malcolm, approaching Jed, could now see his target.

'Calm down, Jed, I'm here to help you,' Malcolm spoke quietly, as he took hold of the fence post and laid it on the ground. Walking on down to the tree line, he bent down and collected the soft toy lion in his arms.

'Must have been dropped here, from a kid's buggy,' he said,

'I'll take it into Betty, in the shop.'

By now, Jeremy had arrived on the scene. Miriam was telling him the whole story. He decided to take Jed into the coffee shop for tea and cake, to calm him down, after first thanking Malcolm for his help.

Tallulah Beaconsfeld remained in the yard with Miriam and Malcolm.

'So sad to see the old man come to this,' she said. 'You know, he's the last of my parents' and Jeremy's grandparents' generation in Cornhaven.

My mother used to talk about how Sir Arthur took him in, after that awful disaster in London, where poor Bethany died. Jed never got over losing her. Irene and I were always just a little bit afraid of him, when we were kids, but I think he's harmless, just very unhappy, at times.'

Jeremy himself accompanied Jed to his doctor's appointment, later that afternoon. Having declared that as Jed had no known living relatives, Jeremy had his own name put down as next of kin, when needed. Doctor Richardson indicated that he would like to book Jed in for further tests, including a more up to date eye examination, before asking to speak to Jeremy privately, while Jed waited outside.

'I'm sorry to have to say this, but I feel Jed is showing signs of dementia,' the doctor reported.

'I will arrange for him to undergo further

tests, but he's done really well to reach almost 93 years. Would he consider a place in residential care, do you think?'

Jeremy was horrified at the thought of the exceptionally independent Jed being placed in a care home.

'No, that won't be necessary, doctor. I'm willing to employ whatever help he needs to keep him in his own place, as long as he remains in reasonable health, physically. Our house-keeper, Ruth, takes him meals and I will arrange other carers to help him, as required.'

'Well, it's up to you,' the doctor replied, 'but things are going to get a lot worse. He really should not be still trying to work.'

Miriam and Jeremy had made a rule that once they were in their master bedroom for the night, anything to do with work remained outside. Still very much in that heady, honeymoon phase, they delighted in making the most of soft sheets and the super king-sized bed that Jeremy had purchased, as soon as they had become engaged.

That night, though, after yet another amazing, passionate embrace, Miriam sensed that Jeremy's mind was wandering.

'Come on, tell me all,' she said.

'It's just this business with Jed,' her husband replied. 'I really can't think what to do for the best, for him.'

'Then you don't really need me to tell you your next move, do you?' Miriam replied. 'Go and talk to Noric, on your own. He's given you good counsel in the past.'

'Miriam, you're a genius!' Jeremy brightened up,

'I'll do exactly that tomorrow evening. In the

meantime - - - - - - -?'

The following evening, Jeremy made his way alone, along the track leading through the metal gate to Noric's world, ancient Cornhaven. The unicorn listened to all he had to say, then appeared to go, head bent down, into a trance. Eventually he raised his head and spoke.

'I sense that Jed's days are numbered. He is not at all well. A week from tonight, I want you to come here again, bringing Miriam and Lady Jane with you.

I will have something to show you all. Thank-you, Jeremy.' With that, Noric turned to walk back to the rest of his herd, leaving Jeremy feeling a little startled. He knew that it had been many years since his mother had spoken with Noric, when Sir Terrance was still alive.

When Jeremy returned to the manor house, he found Miriam laying up the table for dinner in the conservatory, for the three of them.

'Where's my mother?' he asked, after giving Miriam a kiss.

'She should be back very soon,' Miriam replied.

'She went with Ruth to see Jed, in his cottage.'

Just then, his mother's car arrived in the driveway.

Jeremy told them about his visit to Noric, as they enjoyed Miriam's signature coq au vin, served with rice and new bread.

'Jed seemed better, today.' Lady Jane informed them.

'Ruth's staying with him for a while, to make sure he eats some food. Before we all go to see Noric next week, I feel there's something you two should know, concerning Jed. For a start, Jeremy, you've always known him as Jed

Smith. That's not always been his name. He was born Jeremiah Wilberforce-Smythe, Sir Arthur's younger brother. Sir Arthur and Lady Anne took him in as their accountant after other family members rejected him, because of his love for the shop girl, Bethany. Jed was left penniless by his father, all those years ago. You might remember, Jeremy, that he lived here, in this house, when you were small, but preferred to be alone, so Sir Arthur gave him the estate cottage? He's your great uncle, but never wanted to be recognized as such.'

There was silence for a while, until Miriam spoke.

'That's such a sad story. We must do all we can for him, now.'

Jeremy smiled at his wife,

'We will, darling, we will.'

Over the following six days, Jed's behavior continued to be unpredictable. He still insisted on coming into the garden centre, putting the staff very much on the alert. He fell over in the yard, but fortunately only suffered bruises.

On the Wednesday evening, Jeremy, accompanied by Miriam and Lady Jane, kept their appointment with Noric. After greeting them, he asked them to stand back, just into the tree line, as there was something they needed to witness.

They became aware of an intense, white light, descending in front of them. As they watched, it settled on the ground, becoming a pathway, leading into ancient Cornhaven's fir trees. There was a building there, a cottage with a pretty front garden, full of flowers.

'Come forward, Jed,' Noric's soft but commanding voice boomed out. Miriam caught her breath, as the wizened old man appeared, quite close to her, but not able to see the three of them watching him.

'It's time, Jed,' Noric continued. 'Look ahead. Step onto the path.'

Suddenly they saw the door of the cottage open and a beautiful, golden haired girl in a bright gingham frock walked into the garden, smiling towards Jed.

'It's Bethany! My Bethany,' the old man cried out, and immediately started running towards her. With every step he took, the years flew off him, until, once again, he was a young man in his twenties, running towards the girl he loved.

Miriam and Lady Jane had tears in their eyes, as they watched the couple embrace, before heading into the pretty cottage together. Then, as suddenly as it had appeared, the whole image faded away.'

'Jeremy,' Noric began, 'there is work for you to do, on your side of reality. Just know that Jed is now very happy and has found peace at last.'

'Thank-you for letting us see this, Noric,' Jeremy replied. 'It means such a lot to us.'

They left the forest, still feeling stunned, to be met at the manor house by a tearful Ruth.

'He's gone, Lady Jane, he's gone!' she cried.

'The ambulance is at the cottage to take his body away.'

Jeremy ordered the women to go into the manor house and make themselves some tea, while he took his car to Jed's cottage, meeting up with the doctor there. The old man had passed away clasping the one photo he had of Bethany, to his heart.

On   Reflection

The next day, Jeremy decided the garden centre would stay closed, as a mark of respect, for Jed. As all the full time staff were present, anyway, Jeremy called a meeting in the coffee shop, to explain what had happened, without, of course, mentioning Noric and the vision in the forest It was explained that Jed had been related to the family and his memorial would bear his full name, Jeremiah Henry Wilberforce-Smythe. There were gasps of surprise when this was announced.

Reverend Patricia called, in to offer prayers and solace to all who needed her help. Miriam had phoned her, saying that she would not be attending choir practice that evening, after what had happened. Lucas and Piers were totally surprised, as they had not realized that 'the Mole's' behavior was largely due to his illness, when he kept spying on them and the rest of the staff.

Ruth and Jeremy later went over to Jed's cottage, to check that there was nothing perishable there, before locking it up securely, until it was possible for the solicitors to deal with probate.

Ruth was to keep a key to the cottage, so she could check it through, from time to time, before they were in a position to remove personal items and, if necessary, furniture.

In just over a week, once more the garden centre was closed, as the funeral took place in Cornhaven parish church. About sixty villagers attended, as many of them had known the old man at the garden centre for many years, although he rarely spoke to them! Reverend

Patricia conducted the service followed by burial in the family's plot in the churchyard. She gave a short but inspired address, saying how much Jed's work had meant to him and the best anyone could do to respect his memory was to carry on their own work, with his level of dedication.

Later that week, Lady Jane, Jeremy, Miriam and Ruth were called into the family's solicitors' office, for the reading of Jed's will. There was a generous cash gift for Ruth, in recognition of her kindness.

Jed had left Miriam his collection of rare, old, valuable, botanical books, with amazing illustrations, many hand painted, as she had previously admired them, in his office.

But the majority of the estate was to be divided equally between Lady Jane and Jeremy, with a footnote saying he hoped a certain amount could be used for charitable purposes. Jeremy had no idea how much money was involved, so was quite shocked to learn it was in excess of one million pounds!

'I suppose he rarely spent anything on himself,' Lady Jane commented. 'We will give the money careful thought. Perhaps there is something the village needs?'

As the days passed, Lady Jane and Jeremy worked their way through Jed's old office. It had been many years since his accountancy skills were really needed, as they employed an outside firm to help keep the books straight, but mostly Jeremy did this work himself. As Lady Jane preferred the outlook of Jed's old office, with windows towards the manor house grounds and forest, she decided to take it over, leaving her own office, next door to Jeremy's, to Miriam.

Jeremy approved of the move, after asking Miriam if she was happy.

Betty and Malcolm were standing close to the shop entrance, just customer watching.

'Well!' Betty began, 'whatever will happen next? In less than three months we've had a wedding, break-in, and poor old Jed's funeral. Now I suppose I should be getting the shop ready for our Christmas display!'

'That's true,' Malcolm replied. 'Lauren's potted Christmas trees came in this week and it won't be long before we take delivery of the cut ones. Last week in November, I think. Wonder if Jeremy will hold a staff Christmas party this year?'

'Yes, I expect so. Look out, here comes the 'pot lady.' I'd better alert Lauren,' Betty continued.

The 'pot lady,' Maureen, was a regular customer, so called because she invariably approached staff with the words, 'I'm looking for something to go in a pot.' Lauren was alerted and sighed. Quite frankly, she was running out of ideas.

Most customers with outdoor tubs or planters, would be happy with brightly flowering bedding plants, in the summer months and polyanthus or violas through the winter months, but Maureen was different, always on the look-out for something rare or unusual.

Suddenly, Lauren had a brainwave. Walking through Miriam's houseplant department that morning, she had noticed a fresh delivery, boxes of Winter Cherry or Solanum, full of bright orange berries against dark evergreen foliage. The plants themselves were not overly large, but three planted together would make a good

display and the plants themselves were surprisingly hardy, in that part of the south coast. Maureen was happy with her choice,
buying six plants to place in two large pots, beside her front door. One up on the neighbor's! Lauren explained that the berries would not last forever and could be poisonous, but Maureen did not seem to mind, loving the bright orange colour.

Clive was doing well, on his degree course in Bath. He had managed to come back for Jed's funeral and Jeremy had promised him holiday employment, whenever he wanted it. He hoped to be there for two weeks in the run up to Christmas and a week afterwards.

Lauren now had another gap year student to train, Ben, who was not at all sure what he wanted to do as a career, although he had good A levels.

A quiet lad, but also a bit of a dreamer, Ben needed prompting frequently, to make sure he kept working. Before they knew it, a huge lorry arrived, loaded with Christmas trees. Lauren had cleared almost half of the shrub beds and potted trees, to make room for them.

Ben found himself having to think on his feet, as he was now working as part of the team, alongside Alan, Malcolm, Lauren and one of the part time staff, to unload the lorry and carefully line out the trees in order of type, size and price, against wires installed by Alan and Jeremy. Surprisingly, Ben did quite well and there were no major mistakes made.

'We'll make a yardman out of you yet, lad!' Malcolm laughed, throwing some broken branches across to him, to be bunched up for sale.

Later, after dinner, Lady Jane and Miriam were sitting either side of a blazing log fire, with Hector lying on the rug between them. Lady Jane was sipping her customary glass of red wine, while Miriam stuck to tea. Jeremy was clearing plates, pots and pans into the dishwasher, in Lady Jane's kitchen.

'You know, Miriam,' Lady Jane began, 'going into the forest to see Noric again brought back memories. The first time I went there, was with Sir Terrance. By the time we came back, I was expecting Jeremy!'

As her eyes met Miriam's, both women burst out laughing.

'Nothing new there, then, Lady Jane!' Miriam giggled.

'Miriam, please call me Janice,' her ladyship replied. She had become seriously fond of her daughter-in-law, and was really looking forward to seeing her first grandchild.

Preparing for Christmas.

Malcolm had taken Ben under his wing and was showing him how to use the Christmas tree netting machine, which was not a machine at all, just a very large funnel on a stand. Skeins of plastic netting were placed over the outside of the funnel and a tree fed into the wide end, cut end first, pointing towards the narrow end, where the netting was tied in a knot.

As Ben pulled the cut end through the funnel, the netting coated the tree's branches, pulling them together and making it easier to load the whole tree into a car boot, after the net was cut off level with the top of the tree.

Lauren was glad to have both Clive and Clare back, to help with the Christmas rush. Clare had been off work for a month, nursing her mother, who had undergone surgery. Miriam had pre-booked cyclamen, orchids and poinsettias, for the end of November and Clare was more than happy to display and care for them. Clive got on well with Ben, as he recognized him from the year below him at sixth form college.

Betty and her four shop assistants were working flat out, opening boxes, unpacking goods, restocking shelves and answering customers' questions, as they worked.

Jeremy liked his garden centre to have a proper autumn season, before displaying Christmas goods. Lauren decided to keep Alan's flowerpot men figures on display under the covered area in the yard, but surrounded them with topical plants, including variegated ivies, berried potted holly bushes, hellebores in flower and the sweet scented sarcococca or Christmas Box shrub, smothered in white flowers.

Piers and Lucas generally had a quieter time through the Christmas season, mainly focusing on selling lighting for outdoor use. Lucas was busy thinking ahead and collecting together various materials for his part in constructing the Chelsea flower show display garden, for his business associates, the following May.

Amidst the general chaos, Lauren was called by Rachel, requesting a pre-Christmas gardening advice session for her Tuesday afternoon show. Luckily, this one was to be pre-recorded, so Lauren decided to concentrate on giving ideas for gardeners' presents, both plants and shop goods, including tools and books, as well as how to choose and care for houseplants.

She would need to do live sessions from January onwards, including answering listeners' questions on the air.

Jeremy usually gave his staff a proper break over Christmas, meaning that most of them would take a week out of their annual leave then. Two or three might choose to come into work, just for one or two days, between Christmas and New Year, to make a start on preparing unsold Christmas goods for a January sale, as well as removing any remaining cut trees from the yard, while the garden centre was closed to customers.

The staff Christmas party was arranged at the manor house for the day before Christmas Eve. Lady Jane's suggestion of employing the same caterers they had for the wedding reception was agreed and booked well in advance, except that this time it would be a cold buffet, laid on in the main reception room and everyone could help themselves. Jeremy invited Richard and his wife over, too, as he thought some help in serving the drinks might come in handy! Everyone had a great time. Nothing too formal or 'stuffy' was allowed.

It was a chance to chat and catch up on the year's events. They raised a glass to Jed's memory and Jeremy was able to thank everyone for their wholehearted support, in making the business such a success.

He had special words of thanks for Lauren, who had doubled the profits of the garden plants department with her careful buying and promotions, Betty, for maintaining high standards in the shop, along with her staff and Piers and Lucas, again for good sales figures, wishing them good luck with the Chelsea show garden.

'And I can't let this evening go by, without thanking Malcolm and Alan, for standing in for me, when those men broke into the yard,' Jeremy added. 'Malcolm, as you already know, we are now in a position to offer young Alice a full catering apprenticeship here, in the coffee shop, with day release studies at the college from February onwards, if she is happy to give it a go. Also, as my thank-you to you, personally, I would like to send the three of you on holiday in Wiltshire this summer. How does a week at a resort near Longleat Safari Park sound?'

Alice gave a great cheer, as her parents thanked Jeremy profusely.

'As for Alan, congratulations to you and Jenny on your engagement! My friend, Richard, is offering you two a week in Brittany at the farmhouse or gite owned by him and his wife.

'Perhaps it would make a good honeymoon location?' Jeremy suggested.

'What a brilliant idea! Thank-you Jeremy and Richard,' Alan replied. 'Our wedding's booked for July, so that will be just perfect!'

By 10pm, Miriam, her baby bump now quite obvious, was ready to turn in for the night and their guests were gradually leaving. It was a clear, cold night and everyone was wondering if they might see snow on the coast, although it did not happen very often.

Miriam and Jeremy said goodnight to everyone in the main hall, at the foot of the wide staircase, where they had a large, fresh, Christmas tree, from their own forest, decorated with a myriad of golden, twinkling lights.

On Christmas Eve, it was traditional for all of them to go to midnight mass at Cornhaven church. Once again, Joanne, back from university, joined her mother, to sing in the choir.

She had agreed to stay on at the manor house from Christmas Eve until the day after Boxing Day, to help her mother with the meals, as Ruth would be away, taking a hotel break, with her sister.

Christmas Eve was magical, with all the favourite, traditional carols being sung by choir and congregation, some of them by candlelight. As the service ended, they left the church in a flurry of snowflakes. It was, just about, a white Christmas, after all.

The whole family, Lady Jane, Jeremy, Miriam, Joanne and Miriam's parents, Irene and Bill, were together, in front of a crackling log fire on Christmas Day morning, to open their presents. Miriam was only just starting to get ready for the new baby and was pleased to accept gifts for the nursery, mainly pictures, baby blankets and a mobile, to hang over the cot. Later they all enjoyed a perfectly cooked, traditional roast turkey dinner with champagne and all the trimmings.

Joanne had put herself on 'pet duties,' going down to the garden centre to make sure Willow had enough food, in his greenhouse home and then taking Hector for short walks, along with Irene for company.

Meanwhile in Romsey, Lauren and Mark had visitors over Christmas, too. Lauren's parents came up from the South Hams, to stay over and Mark's mother also spent Christmas Day with them. Oliver, of course, got spoiled rotted with expensive presents from his grandparents! Mark's younger sister lived in Australia.

They spoke over a video link on Christmas Day. Lauren had to admit she envied their 'beach barbecue' Christmas, just a little bit. Mark's mother, Diane, had plans to spend the next Christmas with her daughter, Emma, who was now married and expecting her first baby in May.

Into the New Year.

January was not and never had been, Lauren's favourite time of the year. For a start, it was the month for serious stock-taking at the garden centre with much labeling, counting and accounting to be done, at what was a relatively quiet time for the trade, once the January sales were over.

Then there was the cold weather to contend with, having to protect potted plants from frost damage, at the same time as keeping the area looking attractive for customers.

On the plus side, pots of spring-flowering bulbs were coming in from the suppliers, with their attractive picture labels giving people hope for the new season ahead.

Miriam was getting more restless, spending afternoons shopping with her mother, Irene, looking at baby clothes and loose fitting tops for herself. Joanne was back at university once more, promising her Mum that she would be down again, when the baby arrived.

Miriam's due date was 30th March, according to her most recent scan, but she was convinced the baby would arrive sooner. Jeremy's 40th birthday would be on 25th March and there were two more family birthdays before this, Miriam's own on 15th February and Joanne's on 2nd March, but she would most likely not be at home this year for her 19th birthday.

Jeremy had made some changes to the bedroom next to the master suite, to make a comfortable nursery, including an extra door between the two rooms, which each had their own en suite bathrooms. The decorators put up new wallpaper with nursery rhyme figures in mainly pastel shades. Buttermilk woodwork and a warm, cream carpet completed the picture.

On Miriam's birthday, Jeremy booked a table for just the two of them at his friend Richard's restaurant in Bournemouth. As usual, Richard's staff took good care of them, serving the most delicious food, but this time it was a very cold night and Miriam was happy to go straight home, afterwards.

Later that night, as they lay in bed, Jeremy's right hand feeling his baby kicking in his wife's tummy, he had an idea about the money Jed had left them.

'Miriam, what do you think about creating a new children's play park, in that field next to the garden centre car park?' he asked.

'You know, it used to be used to grow trees, for sale in the winter months, but now only Zoe's ponies use it occasionally for grazing. There's over three acres, altogether.'
Miriam was drifting off to sleep. 'Whatever you say, darling, but best ask your mother, first, then the village hall committee. It backs onto their land, after all.' With that, they both fell asleep.

Hector had got used to having Miriam around. Every morning, about 9am, he would be waiting for her in the conservatory, lead in mouth, ready for his walk around the manor grounds or along the drive, as far as the garden centre entrance and back.

February brought snowdrops, early daffodils, scented flowers on the Daphne odora bushes and the odd early
camellia flower, in the gardens. Some weekday mornings, they would stop and chat with Tom, busy tidying flower beds or sweeping paths around the house. If she felt energetic, Miriam walked Hector as far as her old cottage, with its

own pretty garden, now also cared for by Tom. The cottage had once belonged to Miriam's late grand-parents, and she was glad that Joanne would now have it, so it would stay in the family.

Jeremy said he thought of the cottage as their own 'secret retreat,' at least until Joanne was ready to live there, full time.

Jeremy and his mother decided to push ahead with plans to create a new play area for the village children, which would also benefit the garden centre. Discussions on planning permission were taking place.

The village hall committee had no immediate objections, but access from the village side and the garden centre end had to be worked out.

Lauren knew of an excellent play park equipment, construction and installation company, in Devon, which Jeremy contacted for an initial quote. Of course, he wanted the very best for Cornhaven, as it would be a lasting memorial to Jed and the whole Wilberforce-Smythe family.

By early March, the weather was a little milder, if more windy and showery. Gardens were bursting with daffodils, crocuses and early wild primroses. Trade was picking up at the Unicorn, with orders for hanging-baskets already coming in, work normally carried out through April and May, ready for the summer season. Clare was keen to do her part in planting up the summer displays, taking the work load off Miriam, whose baby would arrive very soon. However, not everyone was happy with this change.

One afternoon Miriam, resting at home, received a frantic phone call from a hassled Betty, in the shop.

'So sorry to bother you, Miriam, but I've got Mrs. Pocock here in the shop, insisting on speaking to you, personally, about her hanging-basket order. I've told her Clare is more than happy to do them, but she only wants you. I don't think she believes me when I say you are due to have your baby.'

'Don't worry, Betty. I'll come over.' Miriam replied. Mrs. Pocock was standing by the shop tills, when Miriam's baby bump followed by Miriam, entered.

'Oh dear! Oh dear! I thought your colleague was just fobbing me off!' Mrs. Pocock exclaimed, as Miriam stood smiling at her. 'I'm terribly sorry, but you ALWAYS do my hanging-baskets and I didn't want anyone else.'

'That's fine, Mrs. Pocock,' Miriam replied.

'Once this little one is born, all being well, I hope to get back to doing some of the orders. If you don't mind having yours done a little later, I'm sure it won't be a problem. I have trained Clare though, to make them up exactly as I do.'

'No, no, don't worry, later will be fine. Hope all goes well with the baby,' Mrs. Pocock hurriedly said, as she left the shop.

Miriam wrote the order in her book, which she handed to Clare, before staggering back to the house.

Spring deliveries generally were arriving thick and fast at the Unicorn. Lauren was delighting in new trees, shrubs, perennials and fresh batches of primroses, polyanthus and pansies. Alan's yard was busy receiving pallets of compost, stone, pots and garden ornaments, as well as shop goods for Betty and Piers, which he brought through, one pallet at a time, on a hand operated pallet truck. Lucas now had just about everything he needed, put to one side, ready for the Chelsea show garden.

The evening before Jeremy's fortieth birthday, Miriam felt the first twinges.

She decided to keep this to herself, as it was hardly proper labour pains, made herself a hot chocolate drink and went to bed as normal. At 6am, Jeremy woke to see the light on, in their en suite.

'Up you get, darling,' Miriam said, 'time to go. I've already phoned the maternity hospital, to let them know we're on our way!'

'What! Just like that! Are you really sure?' he asked, hurriedly getting dressed.

Miriam was booked into the private maternity hospital at Barton-on-Sea, for the birth, about three miles from their home. Jeremy quickly grabbed Miriam's case, helping her down the stairs and into his car, waiting on the driveway. By 6.30am, they were in the hospital and heading for the delivery suite.

If she was in a lot of pain, it hardly showed, until about an hour later, when, with Jeremy supporting her head and shoulders, with one terrific push, their baby was born, shouting loudly.

'A beautiful baby boy,' midwife Sonia announced.

'Perhaps the proud father would like to cut the cord,' a booming voice behind them announced, as obstetrician professor Hugh Meredith entered the room, having been told earlier that the Wilberforce-Smyth's baby was on its way. In a daze, Jeremy did as he was shown, by sister Sonia. The midwife wrapped his son in a soft towel, handing the baby to Jeremy, to show to Miriam, whose arms were outstretched towards the baby.

'Do we have a name?' Sonia asked.
Jeremy and Miriam smiled at each other, over their little son's head. 'Nicholas,' they both said together. (Well, with a choice of Ron or Nic, they had decided Nic was the better option!)

'Yes, Nicholas Jeremy,' Miriam added.

After a few, short minutes gazing at this wonderful, miraculous new life that had entered the world, the professor suggested to Jeremy that they 'leave the women to it,' for a few minutes, and took Jeremy into his office, where there was a tray of tea and biscuits waiting for them.

'Congratulations, Sir Jeremy,' professor Hugh began, 'Once upon a time, I would offer new dads a cigar, but I'm afraid that's rather gone out of fashion, now, so only tea. Oh, and happy birthday, by the way!'

'I certainly can't forget this one!' Jeremy replied.

'Now, just a couple of things to say,' the professor continued, as they sipped their tea,

'Firstly, I hope you will agree to your wife spending some time recovering here, with my team taking care of her and your new son. I suggest about five days.

She is in good health, but as an older mother may need more recovery time. Also, I like my ladies to be allowed the full six weeks recovering from giving birth, so no hanky-panky until that time is up and we've given her a full bill of health. Is that clear?'

'Yes, that's fine,' Jeremy replied. I want Miriam and our baby to have the best care possible.'
Just then, there was a tap on the office door.

'Ah good,' professor Hugh said, 'Your wife and son are ready for you now, in their own room.'

'This way, please, Sir Jeremy,' nurse Amy said, leading him towards the lift, 'Your wife and son are in our Magnolia Suite. It looks out over the sea, to the Isle of Wight.'

Miriam was sitting up in bed, baby Nic in her arms, smiles beaming out to her husband.

'Happy Birthday, Darling,' she giggled.

'I'll leave you two alone,' nurse Amy smiled, 'Just call if you need anything.'

Jeremy gently lifted their baby from Miriam's arms, kissing her gently, as he did so.

'What a wonderful birthday present you've given me,' he said, tears in his eyes.

The baby in his arms opened his eyes briefly.

'Hello, Nic!' they both said joyfully.

'Friday's child is loving and giving,' Miriam quoted from the old nursery rhyme, 'so he's going to be just like his Dad!'

Before leaving them, after another hour had gone by, Jeremy got nurse Amy to take some photos of their new son, to show the folks back home.

Miriam had already called Joanne, Irene and Bill and Jeremy phoned his mother before leaving the hospital, letting her know she now had a grandson, weighing in at a healthy eight pounds.

Before going home, Jeremy stopped off in New Milton, as the shops were now open, getting some prints from his camera and ordering a huge bouquet of spring flowers, for his wonderful wife.

As he entered the drive, going past the garden centre entrance, he saw two banners had been put up, one saying

'Happy Birthday,' and the second one proclaiming 'It's a Boy!' He needed to go home first, before seeing the staff.

Within minutes, Jeremy was sat at the table in his conservatory, opposite Lady Jane, with Ruth bringing him a full English breakfast. Hector looked on, soulfully, missing Miriam, until Tom arrived to take him for his walk. A pile of birthday cards and several presents were handed to Jeremy, as everyone gazed at the photos taken by nurse Amy. Lady Jane picked out the largest print, an eight by six inch one of the family of three, to place in one of her photo frames, with Jeremy's permission.

By two pm, Jeremy had been showered with congratulations from all of the staff. Malcolm and Alan said they hoped he would go down to the Fisherman's' Rest with them later, to 'wet the baby's head!'

Miriam's hospital room was full of the scent of spring flowers. She had enjoyed a lovely lunch and had managed to give baby Nicholas his first feed, too.

Her parents visited later in the afternoon, bringing more flowers and fruit, plus a message from Joanne to say she would be down the next day, Saturday, to meet her new baby brother, but would have to go back on Sunday. Irene insisted Joanne should stay overnight at their house, in New Milton.

Jeremy took his mother to briefly visit His wife and baby, during the afternoon. Lady Jane was totally mesmerized with the sight of her grandson, saying how much he was like Jeremy, as a baby. Her sister, Cerys, and the other Welsh relatives sent congratulations and hoped to come down sometime near Easter, to see little Nicholas.

Spring   Progress.

In no time at all, the days had flown and it was time for Jeremy to bring his wife and son back home. It took a few minutes to master the intricacies of fitting the baby safety seat in the back of his car, in the right position for a newborn.

On the way home, Miriam insisted on stopping at the garden Centre entrance. In a few minutes, they were surrounded by congratulating staff, admiring little Nicholas, asleep in his baby seat. Betty and Lauren had some baby presents for Miriam, a musical toy roundabout and a soft toy dog.

Ruth was happy to put in some extra time preparing meals, as she said, the new mother must eat properly. Miriam soon settled herself and the baby into the routine of feeds, meals for herself and midwife or district nurse visits.

At the same time, it now looked as though there were no objections at all to Jeremy's plans for a children's play area to go ahead. In the end, they had decided on dividing the field up, into four sections, with a football field sized area, at the back of the village hall, to be left as open grassland for sport and dog-walking.

There would be a fenced-in children's play park, with a wooden fort climbing frame, slide, several swings, see-saw and roundabout, as well as seating for adults. At the far side of this area,
 there would still be a much smaller paddock, for Zoe's ponies and closest to the garden centre drive, they planned a display garden with more seating and a water feature. Lucas was keen to

use his design skills on this section. A new footpath, either paved or ideally tarmacked,
would run through from the village hall to the garden centre drive.

Two weeks later, it was the Easter holidays. Joanne was back at home from university, staying in the cottage, but enjoying going out with her mother, taking the baby for walks, in his new pram.

Reverend Patricia had been to visit them a few times, but Miriam and Jeremy wanted to wait until June for Nicholas' baptism, as the baby's demands for feeding were somewhat irregular!

Miriam had been looking at helping Clare with the hanging-basket orders and Jeremy had added some screening to part of the old glasshouses, to give her some comfort and privacy if the baby demanded a breast-feed. Somehow, he had also managed to plumb in an old kitchen sink unit, so she had water, to wash her hands.

As they already had chairs and a socket for an electric kettle, Clare declared it a 'home from home,' as she worked with Miriam.

Both Miriam and her son got a clean bill of health from professor Hugh, at their six week check-up and she was told he could see no reason why she could not have another baby, if she wanted, but recommended a two year break.

This made Miriam smile, because one baby was certainly all she could cope with, lovely as he was. So far, she had resisted Jeremy's idea of employing a nanny, but was beginning to see that there could be advantages.

Eventually, things became easier. At seven weeks old baby Nic was mostly sleeping through the night and his baptism was arranged for the last Sunday in May, which would have been the old Whitsun holiday. Richard and Celeste had already agreed to be godparents, plus Miriam had also asked friends from the church choir, Matt and Naomi, because she was their daughter's godmother and liked the idea of having godparents who were involved with Cornhaven parish church. Jeremy readily agreed with this.

Of course, first there was the Chelsea flower show to work towards. Arrangements were made to collect the plants, which had been pre-booked, from several nurseries. Once everything was at the garden centre, the main landscape company creating the show garden, Cornhaven Garden Design, came over to inspect, collect and load everything for the London show.

Lucas would travel up and stay with them, for the build, until after judging took place. Jeremy was anxious to ensure that the Unicorn would be credited with giving assistance with the show garden and intended going there himself, once judging was finished.

Lauren, Mark and Oliver would visit the show on the first members' day, followed by Piers and Lucas at the weekend.

It turned out to be a great success. Cornhaven Garden Design were rewarded with their first ever gold medal! Lucas and Jeremy were beaming with happiness at the result. Once again, the Unicorn got a good write up in the local paper, along with a photograph of Lucas, Jeremy and the landscapers, in front of their prize-winning show garden.

Lauren was celebrating her first complete year, working at the Unicorn, delighted with her own success. Jeremy had rewarded Lauren with a good cash bonus in April, saying that he hoped she would be with them for a good many years to come. May month had been busier than ever and Clare had proved a great help to Lauren, with Miriam's time being taken up by baby Nicholas.

When it came to customers like Mrs. Pocock, Clare and Miriam divided up the order between them, in Mrs. Pocock's case, they did three hanging baskets each, all identical. Lauren remarked that no-one could tell the difference. Jeremy promoted Clare to supervisor, as she was now taking care of all the houseplants and bedding plants, but Miriam still did the buying, alongside Lauren.

Full   Circle.

Baby   Nicholas   Jeremy   was   baptised   or christened   at   Cornhaven   parish   church,   on   the last   Sunday   in   May,   with   all   the   family   present, including   his   half-sister   Joanne   and   also   Lady Jane's   Welsh   relatives.

They   opted   for   the   Sunday   afternoon,   as Miriam   thought   adding   the   ceremony   to   the morning   service   might   be   a   step   too   far   for   most of   them,   but   she   promised   Reverend   Patricia   that the   baby   would   be   in   church   the   following Sunday,   with   both   his   parents,   for   a   blessing   at the   altar.

The   baby   beamed   a   smile   at   the   vicar,   as she   took   him   to   the   font,   followed   by   a   yell, when   he   felt   the   water   on   his   head,   although   it had   been   warmed.

He   was   congratulated   and   greatly   admired   by all   and   was   generally   well   behaved,   being passed   from   one   to   another.   It   was   not   strictly   a private,   family   service.

All   parishioners   were   invited,   with   tea   laid   on in   the   village   hall,   rather   than   the   smaller   church hall,   because   the   family   were   not   sure   just   how many   might   turn   up!   Jeremy   and   Miriam   had done   the   traditional   thing   of   saving   the   top   layer of   their   wedding   cake   for   the   christening   party, although   Julie   had   baked   a   second   one,   just   in case!

Lady   Jane,   or   Janice,   as   her   friends   now called   her,   was   sitting   alone,   towards   the   back of   the   village   hall,   when   Rev.   Patricia   noticed and   joined   her   there.

'Your   family   looks   so   very   happy,'   the   vicar began,   'and   that   little   baby   grandson   is   a   real treasure.   Joanne   looks   happy   too,   talking   to   her step-dad. They could almost be father and daughter.'

'Or, uncle and niece!' Lady Jane commented, causing a surprised glance, from the vicar.

'My late husband was known in the village for straying from his marriage vows. Last week , I found a photo,' Lady Jane continued. 'It was of Sir Terrance's mother, Anne, taken around Joanne's age. She looked so much like Joanne. I've my suspicions that Miriam's first husband, David, was my late husband's son. Jeremy would have been David's half-brother!'

Just then, they were joined by Rev. Patricia's husband, Victor, who taught history at the sixth form college.

'Do I hear hints of a scandal?' he asked, somewhat jovially. 'There's always a lot going around in villages!'

'Now, now, Victor,' his wife protested, 'just look at them. Joanne obviously loves that little baby, almost as much as her mother. I've never seen such a happy family group.

So much love there. What does the past matter, anyway? Lady Jane, Janice, you are so very lucky to have them, truly Heaven blessed.'

'Thank-you. I know that's true,' her ladyship replied, leaving the table, to speak to her sister, Cerys.

Miriam had noticed a tall man she did not recognise, in the hall, standing next to Cerys and Bryn.

'Jeremy, do you know that man?' she asked.

'Turns out he's Bryn's older brother,' Jeremy replied. 'He's a widower. Met my mother in Bournemouth last year, after our wedding, when they all went to the theatre together. I think Mother said he is a retired accountant, moved to Hampshire from Wales some years ago.'

'That's interesting,' Miriam smiled, 'he seems to be getting on very well with Janice this afternoon!'

Lauren and Mark made it down to Cornhaven for the christening, bringing Oliver with them, who was happy to meet up with Richard and Celestes' children, Molly and Marcus, once more. The children headed outdoors to play, while the adults talked.

'Makes me feel quite broody, seeing Miriam with that gorgeous baby boy,' Lauren said, dreamily, to Mark.

'Well, it's not too late for us, if we did decide to give Oliver a little brother or sister,' Mark replied. 'After all, am I right in thinking you are a few years younger than Miriam?'

'I know,' Lauren replied, 'but on the other hand, I am really enjoying my work here and would be sad to give it up, right now. It is a steady income for us, too.'

'There is something I haven't told you,' Mark said, looking a little worried. 'You know you told me about that horticultural officer's post in Lymington? Well, I put in an application and I've been called in for an interview, later this week. If it come off, we could think about moving this way.'

'What! I thought you enjoyed being self-employed,' Lauren exclaimed.

'Yes, but it is unpredictable, when it comes to income and maybe, after ten years, I should be thinking more about our future. Besides, it gives me a chance to make further use of my degree, as the work mostly involves planning and advising other people, especially schools in the area, which I know I would love to do, after all, you now do those radio broadcasts regularly, giving advice.' Mark had barely drawn breath, in his enthusiasm.

Baby Nicholas had done very well for christening presents. Godparents Richard and Celeste presented him with a silver tankard, engraved with his full name and the date and place of his baptism. Matt and Naomi gave Miriam and Jeremy a beautiful, pictorial, children's Bible, for the start of his Christian journey.

There were presents of baby clothes and soft toys, as well as over forty cards, marking the day. Miriam intended to keep them all, mounted in a scrap book with photos taken throughout the afternoon.

Miriam decided she wanted to know more about the 'mystery man' at the party, Bryn's brother, who was paying quite a lot of attention to her mother-in-law. She decided Cerys would be the best bet, for a proper introduction and carried the baby over to her.

'Oh, Miriam!' Cerys began, such a wonderful day, lovely baby and isn't he good? I don't think you've been introduced to my brother-in-law. This is Bevan, he's a chartered surveyor, but mostly retired now, living in Bournemouth.'

'Which is where I had the pleasure of meeting Janice last year, when the four of us went to see 'Blythe Spirit' at the theatre,' Bevan added, smiling. 'I'm hoping she might consider spending some more time with me, this summer. I have a villa in the South of France.'

'Sounds wonderful,' said Miriam, 'let's hope it all works out for you.'

Returning to Jeremy and Joanne, Miriam told them of her conversation with Bevan.

'Perhaps we should be making plans for a holiday, later this summer,' Miriam wondered.

'Sorted!' Jeremy grinned. 'How do you feel about returning to the Isles of Scilly in September? Of course, this time it will be a cottage for four.'

'Four?' Miriam queried.

'Yes, Joanne's agreed to come as well, to be our baby-sitter. What do you think?' Jeremy asked. Joanne was smiling.

'Absolutely wonderful!' Miriam replied. 'Thank-you, Joanne.'

By the end of June, the new children's play area was almost complete. The Devon based company recommended by Lauren had done an amazing job. Jeremy was very favourably impressed by their workmanship, especially the large wooden fort which was a combination of climbing frames and slides.

Some of the equipment was suitable for use by less physically able children, with a roundabout that could take wheelchairs and a circular, hammock or cradle-shaped large swing.

The ground had previously been re-levelled and re-turfed, with safety surfacing beneath all the play equipment. Six benches for adult observers were placed around the outside, against the fence. Once completely finished, with everything checked for health and safety, it would be opened for the children's use.

Meanwhile, Lucas and Lauren, with some help from Ben, were working together on the display garden area, nearest the garden centre drive. Lucas installed a shallow, pre-formed pond, suitable for wildlife, with a small waterfall cascading into it, solar powered, when the sun shone.

Lauren wanted to show off and promote many of their bestselling plants and included good evergreens, Ceanothus, Eleagnus, Abelia, Escallonia, Camellias, which would tolerate some lime and Daphne odora, for its outstanding scent in early spring. She included hardy herbs, rosemary, thyme and lavender plus some deciduous shrubs including Forsythia, for early flowers, Weigela, Viburnum Bodnantense and a selection of Hydrangeas for summer flowering. Between them, Lucas and Lauren worked in a winding, narrow paved path with an arch, over which Lauren was growing an Albertine rose and a white-flowering Clematis.

There was space for two arbour seats and half a dozen stoneware pots, to take alpines or tender perennials in the summer months. Pride of place was a memorial plaque, mounted on a large granite rock, saying that the whole area was dedicated to Jeremiah Wilberforce-Smythe, with thanks for his legacy to the community.

Jeremy and Miriam were spending more time working together, in Miriam's new office, as Jeremy wanted her to understand more about the financial side of the business. That particular afternoon, young Nicholas decided he was hungry, just after they had finished discussing the previous month's takings.

Miriam undid her top to feed the baby, watched by her husband, amazed by just how fast the baby was growing, on his mother's milk. However, at times, you could say Jeremy found it a little 'disturbing.'

'You OK, Jeremy?' Miriam asked.

'Yes,' he replied, 'but it does make me want to whisk you off to bed!'

'Mmmm,' she said. 'I know how you feel. My midwife said women get like this because of the hormones released with breast feeding.

' Never mind, we won't need to stop and

plan the   'protection' thing much longer.'

'What do you mean?' he asked.

'Well,' she began, 'you know I had that clinic appointment this morning? I've had it done, fitted straight away, no problem.'

'That's very brave of you. Did it hurt?' Jeremy asked.

'No just a bit of discomfort. Some bleeding. But I'm fine.' She smiled at him, 'I just thought I did not want to go on the pill while I was breast feeding, unless this coil doesn't work out and I wanted it all sorted out well before our holiday in September. So far, so good.'

Later, when Jeremy was out taking Hector for his evening walk, he became aware of the white lights over the forest.

Walking on the drive, towards the new play area, he could see the circular, hammock style swing was moving. Hector refused to walk forward, trying to pull Jeremy away. There was a noise from the forest, through the gathering mists, a sort of combination of a horse neighing and a high pitched yell. Lengthening Hector's lead, Jeremy walked forward to where he could see the play area clearly. There was a white shape sprawled across the swing, moving it to and fro. A white horsey shape with a golden horn?

'Oh no,' Jeremy thought

'not one of Noric's lot!'

Suddenly, young Urni, Noric's youngest colt, must have realised he was being watched, as with a terrific leap, he left the play area and cleared the paddock fence, heading back into the forest. Back to ancient Cornhaven, where his mother, Noni, was calling to him. Once the unicorn had left, Hector walked back to Jeremy, who shortened his lead. Jeremy was unsure what to do, as Noric should already be aware of what had happened.

He decided the only answer was to make regular checks at night, to see if the unicorn returned.

But that was not all. Jeremy noticed a shape in the mist in his path, a woman with long, grey hair, carrying a trug full of leaves - Tallulah! He hesitated for a minute, then decided there was no way of avoiding her.

'Good evening, Tallulah, what are you doing here?' he asked.

'Gathering herbs from the forest. My Ralph has a bad case of gout and the best healing comes from the herbs gathered at the nearest full moon to mid-summer, but I avoid darker nights, because of the forest spirits,' Tallulah replied.

'I think you know, Jeremy, I think your family understands about this forest of yours. I think you saw that unicorn, same as me!'

'Tallulah, there are many mysteries attached to Cornhaven,' Jeremy replied. 'Yes, I saw something cross from the play park to the forest. Could have been a white pony.'

'Jed told us when we were just kids, Irene and me. We used to play in those woods and he said we weren't allowed, because of other worldly things living there. But we saw nothing. Not before tonight,' Tallulah continued.

'I'm sure it was probably a pony,' Jeremy said, trying to calm her down, 'but best keep it to ourselves, as other people might go looking for the animal. I know there are white deer in this part of the New Forest.'

Tallulah stared at him for a moment, then

saying, 'Goodnight,' she headed off home, to her husband.

At the end of June, Lauren, Mark and Oliver were visiting Lauren's parents, once more, in Devon. They liked to go to Bigbury-on-Sea together, when the weather was warm, but before the main holiday season got underway. As Oliver searched through the rock pools at low tide, with his grandparents, Lauren and Mark looked on, a few yards behind them.

'So, you've got the new job,' Lauren said, 'when do you start?'

'Not before August,' Mark replied, 'then I'll be on three months' trial, to see how it works out, but I'm really longing to give it a go. They seem a nice, friendly team, in Lymington.'

'You know the other thing we were talking about?' Lauren began, 'Well, I feel I want another year yet, working at the Unicorn, before thinking about having another baby. I am a lot stronger now than I used to be, but the job's going really well.'

'I think you're right,' Mark said. 'It's not good to go through too many changes at once. Come on, I'll race you over to Burgh Island!'

It was a pleasant, warm summer. Alan and Jenny's wedding, the first Saturday in July, was a lovely day. Nowhere near as grand as Jeremy and Miriam's the previous August, but they still got married in the parish church and had a hotel reception in the New Forest, heading off to Brittany afterwards, for a week's honeymoon at the farmhouse on the coast.

Alice was now well into her apprenticeship, working in the Unicorn's coffee shop. Lucas had helped Cornhaven Garden Design move their prize winning Chelsea show garden to the grounds of a local hospice, where it was being greatly admired by all and bringing more customers to the garden centre.

Lady Jane, Janice, accepted Bevan's kind invitation to join him in his villa, in the South of France, staying almost six weeks. She wanted to be back home before Jeremy and Miriam went away for their holiday, with baby Nicholas and Joanne.

One day in August, busily preparing some baby food for their little one's lunch, Miriam noticed her husband in slightly somber mood.

'What are you thinking?' she asked him.

'I'm thinking we still have one important job to do this month,' he replied. So, later that evening, Jeremy, Miriam and little Nicholas, being carried by his father, headed into the forest, through the metal gate, to visit ancient Cornhaven, together. The baby, awake and wide eyed, soft brown hair moving in the breeze, seemed to be looking intently at everything around him.

'Do you think he'll be able to see them?' Miriam asked.

'We'll soon find out,' Jeremy replied, as the mists cleared in front of them.

Noric's golden horn glinted in the evening sun, as he lifted his head and saw the family watching him. He summoned his herd of six together, leading them up to meet Jeremy, Miriam and the baby. Simultaneously, the unicorns stopped in front of the humans, bowing their heads, reaching their front right hooves forwards. The baby started wriggling excitedly, in Jeremy's arms.

'He CAN see them!' Miriam exclaimed.

'We greet you, and wish you welcome to ancient Cornhaven, young master Nic,' Noric said solemnly.

Suddenly, the baby freed his right arm from his carry blanket and raised his hand to the unicorns, shouting the baby equivalent of 'Yay!'

'He's high-fiving the unicorns!' Miriam laughed. In the background, as the mist cleared further, Jeremy could just see a pretty cottage garden, with a youthful Jed and Bethany also raising their hands in greeting to the future Lord Nicholas Jeremy Wilberforce-Smythe, as Gordon, the green woodpecker, flew past.

Author

Cornish born Kay Hart has had a varied career in horticulture, research, sales and teaching. She is a published author, but this is her first work of fiction.

The story

The Wilberforce-Smythes have taken over the derelict Unicorn public house and an old nursery, to create a very successful garden centre in deepest Hampshire. BUT - - - - what is really behind Jeremy's success? Will Miriam get her man and above all, what on Earth is Jed up to? Kay Hart's whimsical tale of country folk reveals all.

Printed in Great Britain
by Amazon